## "You represent criminals and get them off on technicalities so they can do more damage. Is that a fun thing for you?"

"That's not exactly how it works, but I do represent my clients to the best of my ability, and it's my job to protect their rights and see that they get a fair trial."

"Even if it means letting a murderer go free."

Luke's muscles tightened under his skin. He had to admit he'd done things he wasn't proud of, and this woman must have felt the effects of them.

Before he could respond, Jayden started walking away.

"So you want to tell me what's given you such a negative opinion of public defenders?" he shouted after her.

The scrumptious vet—a title that suited her much better than Jayden—turned, and he could see the tracks of tears on her face.

"My sister was Katelyn Casio."

Dear Reader,

We've all faced difficult decisions in our lives. It's the choices we make that define us. Jayden Miller is someone who's trying to make good decisions, though it often means making her life a little harder. When she meets Luke Taylor, she's afraid choosing love could put her family in danger. I hope you'll enjoy Jayden and Luke's story as I return to one of my favorite places, Cypress Landing, Louisiana.

I love to hear from readers. You can reach me by post at Suzanne Cox, 107 Walter Payton Dr., #271, Columbia, MS 39429, or by e-mail at suzannecox@suzannecoxbooks.com. I hope you'll visit me on the Web at suzannecoxbooks.com, superauthors.com and pinkladiesblog.com.

*Suzanne Cox*

# ONE MAN TO PROTECT THEM

*Suzanne Cox*

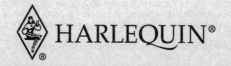

HARLEQUIN®

TORONTO • NEW YORK • LONDON
AMSTERDAM • PARIS • SYDNEY • HAMBURG
STOCKHOLM • ATHENS • TOKYO • MILAN • MADRID
PRAGUE • WARSAW • BUDAPEST • AUCKLAND

ISBN-13: 978-0-373-71462-9
ISBN-10:     0-373-71462-9

ONE MAN TO PROTECT THEM

www.eHarlequin.com

**Printed in U.S.A.**

## ABOUT THE AUTHOR

Suzanne Cox remembers writing her first stories when she was about nine or ten years old. She's been writing ever since. In 2002 she decided to seriously try to get some of her work published. On February 14, 2005, she sold her first book, *A Different Kind of Man,* to Harlequin Superromance. While trying to decide what she wanted to be when she grew up, besides a writer, Suzanne went to college (a lot) and worked a variety of jobs. These days, when not writing, she's at her day job as an allied health instructor at a high school career and technology center. In her spare time, when she can find some, she enjoys reading, painting, biking and fishing. She's presently "livin' my dream" in south Mississippi with her own personal hero husband, Justin, and her boy in puppy dog clothes, Toby, who masquerades as a miniature pinscher.

**Books by Suzanne Cox**

**HARLEQUIN SUPERROMANCE**
1319–A DIFFERENT KIND OF MAN
1389–UNEXPECTED DAUGHTER

To Justin for giving me the confidence to chase my dreams. It's a two-edged sword, I know!

To my mom and mother-in-law
for being my biggest fans.

To the FNGs—you guys are the best.
Where would I be without you!!

To my Bogalusa buddies—we may not win the lottery but we'll sure have fun trying.

# CHAPTER ONE

HER SNEAKERS WET WITH DEW, Jayden lengthened her stride to catch up with Kasey, as the German shepherd bounded into the underbrush, nose to the leaves. Combing the woods for a dead body had become their assignment by default. With the early-morning ringing of the phone while it was still pitch-black outside, Jayden had been inducted into Cypress Landing's volunteer search-and-rescue team. "Volunteer" being the operative word. Coercion would have been more apt. She hadn't bothered to ask how Sheriff Wright had heard about Kasey's talents. Small town, no secrets—she had to keep reminding herself. She'd likely been the topic of conversation even before she'd finally returned home. Estranged hometown girl returns from life in city. She ground her teeth. No time to dwell on that now.

Kasey darted past the massive trunk of an old oak. Damn old Joe Gifford for giving her the cadaver dog and getting her involved in this kind of gruesome insanity. Now, two years later, Joe had passed away, she'd left California, and Kasey was the only thing she had left from her previous life. She thrust aside the damp huckleberry bush, still hanging on to its tiny green leaves. A second flashlight cut an arc beside hers.

"Got anything yet?"

She shook her head. Deputy Fontenot was worried. She couldn't so much see it in the predawn darkness, as she could feel it leaking from his pores right into her own skin. Or maybe blaming her feelings on Pete was her own desperate attempt to remain calm. Just then Kasey pawed at something, then sat on the ground, whining between his low-key barks. When she reached him, she ruffled his red-and-black coat. "Looks like this might be it."

Pete gripped her by the shoulder, and she shivered in her long-sleeve T-shirt.

"It's not your fault."

"If I'd reported him missing sooner we might not be standing here now." She hadn't seen Eric Walsh for a week. This wasn't how she'd hoped to find him.

"I wouldn't have thought it strange that a grown man wasn't home for a few days. Plenty of folks wouldn't have reported it yet."

The yellow cone of his light flashed on the ground as Pete keyed his radio and spoke to some faraway dispatcher. Jayden took a few deep breaths and hoped it wasn't her tenant buried at their feet.

"They're coming," Pete said, readjusting his radio. "But it may be nothing. These leaves are pretty tamped down, and I don't see any fresh earth."

"Kasey wouldn't have made a hit if it was nothing."

"Maybe it's a dead animal."

"He doesn't identify dead animals, only people."

"So maybe he's wrong this time."

She faced Pete, her flashlight still pointed to the spot marked by the dog.

"He's not wrong." She pushed aside some damp leaves with the toe of her boot until the disturbed earth was visible. Pete went to his knees and scraped away more debris.

"I'd never have seen this if I'd been walking by."

"That's the point of the dog."

Voices echoed through the woods behind them and they moved to make room for the sheriff's personnel, armed with shovels, forcing their way around the trees. The first strike of metal into damp earth made Jayden shudder and she leaned against a tree. Kasey whined and rubbed his head against her leg, as she knotted a fistful of his fur then closed her eyes and tried to shut out the thump of the shovel pushing deeper into the ground.

"I got something."

Every person who had pressed into the area froze. No more low chatter speculating why the Saints lost this past Sunday and what Dallas would do with their new quarterback. No more discussion of where the fish might be biting this weekend. They held their collective breath, and Jayden tried not to watch, to not see between the bodies that crowded around the newly opened grave. But she was drawn to the macabre scene in front of her.

The officer digging with the shovel let go of the wooden handle and it bounced on the ground. He dropped to his knees, clawing at the fresh earth. Someone commented that the hole needed to be bigger, but was cut short when the man held aloft the object of their search. Jayden slid to the ground, covering her mouth against the wave of vomit that boiled into her throat. She couldn't seem to block the smell of rotting flesh that immediately assaulted them.

"Jayden." Her eyes closed, she recognized the sheriff's voice. He touched her knee, but she couldn't answer him.

"Jayden, did you ever notice if Eric Walsh wore a watch?"

She nodded, her eyes still jammed shut.

"Would you recognize it if you saw it?"

"Yes," she whispered.

The stench had dispersed into the air, and when she squinted she noticed the first rays of dawn beginning to filter through the trees. The scratched silver watch, with its worn band, appeared in front of her.

"That's Eric's."

"You're sure?"

"I'm sure. He ate dinner with us a lot and he'd always take it off to wash his hands, then forget and leave it by the sink." The last word caught in her throat and tears leaked onto her cheek. "He had a story for how it got each mark. The boys loved hearing his stories." She swallowed hard. "I tried to tell him he was prying into things that would get him into trouble. He didn't listen." She studied a small hole at the hem of her jeans.

"He'd been in Cypress Landing for months before you came. He knew what he was doing. I warned him more than once myself. I'm calling in another team and we'll keep searching on our own. I don't want you to have to keep doing this."

She forced her attention to his face. "What are you saying, Matt? You think there are more bodies?"

The sheriff, squatting beside her, wiped his forehead. "I'm saying that the only thing we've found is one arm."

She tilted her head to rest on her knees and forced herself to breath deeply, but that only made her aware of the scent of decay.

Matt rested his palm on her head. "Why don't you get out of here. My wife's on the road with coffee and food."

She took a gulp of air and shook her head. When she scrambled to her feet, Matt rose with her. "I need to touch base with my mom and let her know to get the kids to school for me. She came over and stayed with them when I left. Then I'll let Jeffrey know I'll be late getting to the office."

"You sure you want to finish this?"

"I want every piece of Eric Walsh found, then I want somebody to pay for putting him here. And I'll do whatever it takes to make that happen."

Six hours later, Jayden stuck a flag in the final section of the property she'd been assigned to search. She'd been joined by three other teams with cadaver dogs. After only a few hits, they figured Eric wasn't the only person buried in these woods. The sun had climbed high and, with the heat and humidity, her clothes were wet with sweat. Shouting for Kasey, she checked her compass and made her way to the roadside where teams of law enforcement and state crime-lab officials scrambled back and forth in the wooded area.

Cecile Wright waved at her, and she hurried to the Wrights' truck, where the sheriff's wife was handing out provisions.

"Who's running the shop for you?"

Cecile had a gift shop and art-supply store on Main Street.

"I closed for the day and came to help. I can't believe what they're finding. Everyone knew Duke Swayze wasn't in his right mind, but this is beyond anything I'd have thought of him."

"Now, Mrs. Wright," a man said from behind Jayden, "I know you aren't automatically assuming Mr. Swayze is responsible."

Jayden sidled round to see who it was. Mid-swallow, she had to gulp to get her water past the tightening in her throat. She'd been away from Cypress Landing for ten years. While many of the faces remained the same, this was a new one. And what a face it was. She wasn't typically impressed or excited about handsome men, but this one had what Hollywood labeled the "wow" factor. He wasn't perfect, with cheekbones and a forehead that bordered on heavy. But he was total man right down to the pullover shirt stretched tight across his chest.

"Luke," Cecile said, "I know representing people like Swayze is what you do, but this is going to be a difficult case."

The man—Luke—shrugged and fished a soda from the ice chest. "Like you say, it's my job." He wiped his hand on his pant leg and held it out toward Jayden. "Luke Taylor, public defender for the parish."

"Jayden Miller."

He engulfed her hand in his warm grasp. His palm was rough, as though he did manual labor, not what she'd expect from a lawyer. He flashed a smile and she smiled back. Cecile apologized for not introducing them, explaining to Luke that Jayden had moved home and was a vet at the local animal clinic. He tilted his head to one side while he held on to her hand for several seconds longer than necessary. For an instant her heart skipped and she got a strange feeling from head to toe. The idea that this man was going to be important flashed through her mind. She'd never fallen for anyone at first sight. She'd always thought it an exaggeration that people invented. But here she was, very attracted to a man who was likely married or being pursued by every available local beauty. She didn't consider herself a beauty or available.

When he let her go, she stuffed her tingling hand in the pocket of her jeans. She didn't have time for this. In California, men had filtered through her life—a few more serious than others—but none she'd allowed herself to get too involved with. Involvement could lead to bad decisions and trouble she didn't need. She mumbled "hello" between sips of water. Crunching on her chips—the thought of eating anything more nauseated her after what she'd seen today—Jayden ignored Cecile and Luke. It must have been his immense sex appeal that had made her foggy, but at last her brain kicked in. She should have realized immediately who this man was, but she'd let his shocking blue eyes and almost too-long brown hair cloud her thinking.

"Public defender? Don't tell me you're defending the guy who did this."

Luke wanted to tell this woman it was all a big mistake. He'd grasped the hand of a woman who'd made his world pause and then she turned on him as if he'd done her a terrible wrong. Honesty was the best policy, right? Which was, of course, a complete joke.

"That's right. He's my client. You don't know with any certainty that he did this, do you?"

"The fact that body parts were scattered across his property doesn't mean anything to you?"

"This is a secluded area. Anyone could have disposed of remains here."

"You must not know Swayze's history or you wouldn't waste your time hunting anyone else."

He likely knew more of Cypress Landing's under-belly than she'd ever imagine. It was an entire other community she likely didn't even know existed.

Luke was much more interested in watching the sparkling gold flecks in her eyes than in discussing the guilt or innocence of his new client. She was a beauty in all the unfashionable ways. The kind who looked good first thing in the morning without makeup, or when she'd come from the deep woods, clothes soaked in sweat with twigs in her dark hair. He took another drink of his soda, still not answering her. When he looked at her he felt a rush of interest stronger than he'd ever known, but his job had to come first.

"I know as much about him as someone who's been gone for…" He paused. "How long?"

"Ten years."

He was surprised she'd responded. Ten years. What had brought her back to this little town in the middle of nowhere after ten years? It was a long time, enough time to build a life somewhere else. He rubbed the back of his neck with the cold soda can. The heat was unbearable for fall.

When he only nodded, she continued to stare at him, her full, sexy lips tense.

"You represent criminals and get them off on technicalities so they can do more damage. Is that a fun thing for you?"

Cecile touched the other woman's arm but she shook it off. He couldn't ignore the anger in her accusation. He also couldn't understand where it came from.

"That's not exactly how things work, but I do represent my clients to the best of my ability and it's my job to protect their rights and see that they get a fair trial."

"Even if it means letting a murderer go free."

Luke's muscles stiffened under his skin. He had to admit he'd done things he wasn't proud of, and this woman must have felt the effects of it.

Before he could respond, she started walking away, saying to Cecile over her shoulder, "I guess I'll go now. I have time to run by the clinic before I pick the kids up from school."

She patted her leg and a German shepherd he hadn't noticed before trotted after her. A vet with kids. She was probably married. Even if she wasn't, kids meant home and stability and a legion of other things he'd avoided so far. He couldn't risk a relationship that would complicate his situation. But his curiosity got the best of him. Luke had to know what had made her so hostile toward him.

"So, you want to tell me what's given you such a negative opinion of public defenders?" he shouted after her. Cecile, he noticed, was shaking her head and staring at the ground.

The scrumptious vet, a title that suited her much better than Jayden, turned and he could see the tracks of tears on her face.

"My sister was Caitland Casio." She turned sharply and hurried away.

"I tried to stop you," Cecile said.

Luke stared at the grass on the side of the road, crushed by vehicles driving over it, then shrugged. "I guess I'd have found out sooner or later. Not exactly my most shining moment, was it?"

"You were doing your job."

He sighed. "I better get back to the office."

The soles of his shoes scuffed against the asphalt. He'd lost so much in his life, but he'd always kept moving, focusing on a goal. Cypress Landing was a good place and he liked it. If things had been different, not now, but in the beginning, when he was a kid, he could have been happy living here. Maybe with an attractive woman like the vet. Buried in this deception, he was beginning to lose track of himself. Occasionally, he wanted to ask for the real Luke to please step forward. Though, he couldn't be certain he'd recognize the guy if he did.

THE WHITE CARD with the huge numbers printed on it reflected in the windshield. Jayden inched her car forward, watching the line of teachers and tiny people streaming from the building. It was how she'd decided to think of the two boys who'd fallen into her lap, waist-high humans. What else could she do? She was much better at dealing with Kasey than she was with two kids both under the age of twelve. For three seconds she contemplated spinning the car around and driving west until she ran into the ocean. But then she saw two curly mops of black hair bobbing as the kids raced toward her, their backpacks nearly toppling them. In the seat behind her, Kasey whined and wagged his tail. Even he was better at this parenting thing than she was. The door flew open and the two piled in, smothering Kasey with hugs. Her, they glanced at cautiously. She had to fight to keep from dropping her forehead to the steering wheel in utter defeat. Jayden had never intended to return to Cypress Landing. Beverly Hills might not have been the home she'd been dreaming of, might not have filled that empty spot she'd felt for ten years, but coming here surely wasn't the answer. She was trapped raising two kids with no idea how to do it.

# CHAPTER TWO

JAYDEN STARED at the breakfast she'd set out before calling the boys. Oatmeal, juice and apple slices—what kind of strange kids were these two? Her mother would have had to sit on her and funnel liquefied oatmeal down Jayden's throat to get her to eat it when she was ten years old. Thankfully, Evette Miller had been more of a biscuits-and-tomato-gravy cook, likely accounting for Jayden's elevated cholesterol count. Her sister had managed to train these boys to eat healthier.

Elbows on the counter, she battled the tightness in her chest. When Caitland and Robert had died in a car crash a few months ago, she'd dropped everything to come and raise their children. Her sister hadn't told her they'd made her legal guardian. But then, who else was there? Their mother couldn't be expected to be responsible for two young boys, not when she was getting ready to retire. Besides, Caitland had wanted Jayden in Cypress Landing for years. She'd always said she'd get her home if it was the last thing she did.

Jayden blinked rapidly, had to fight to get her

breath. At times like this, when the birds sang in the morning air and the light north wind began to make the dimming green leaves wiggle... Her mother would be by soon. She straightened, and prepared to unleash chaos.

"Boys, breakfast!"

She heard squeals from the bedroom, then a thump, followed by the dog barking. The day had officially begun. She spread her feet apart and bent to hug eight-year-old Garrett as he ran into the kitchen. He smiled. It was a start.

"You're dressed and I only came to get you one time. Wow."

"I'm great, huh?"

"You and your brother are the best. I didn't know little boys could be so smart."

Garrett struggled loose, grinning, and scurried to the table. But there was still no sign of Elliot, who at ten deemed himself the man of the house, a title much too overwhelming for a boy. She strode to his room, and found him carefully tying his sneakers. She often wondered if the older brother had come from the womb sporting a pair of neatly double-knotted tennis shoes.

"Ready for breakfast?"

He bobbed his head in a gesture that meant less than nothing to her.

"Anything wrong?"

He shrugged.

"Hmm," she said as he followed her to the kitchen. "Is that yes, no, maybe, I don't know, the dog ate my homework?"

Elliot snorted. "Kasey wouldn't eat my home-work."

"You're probably right. So what's on your mind?"

"We've got baseball practice tonight and tomor-row, then they're going to pick teams."

"I know. I've already made plans to take you."

"But what if I don't get picked to be on a good team?"

"Then you'll be the best player on a not-so-good team."

He slunk into a chair at the table. "You haven't seen me play, Aunt J. How do you know I'll be the best?"

"We've been throwing the ball in the yard every evening, and you're excellent at that. Though I'm mostly going by how the people in the clinic the past few weeks have been asking if you were playing this year and telling me how much they wanted you on their team. I'm guessing you're an outstanding player."

He spooned his oatmeal obviously unimpressed. "I like baseball, a lot. My dad and I—" He paused and swallowed hard. Jayden held her breath. "We played all the time."

"I'll be glad to practice with you."

He snorted then took a bite of his apple. "You're not much help."

She put her fists on her hips, mustering an offended scowl. This was the first time he'd been able to mention his dad without crying. "Maybe this Saturday we should get your friends together and go to one of the fields for a game. I'll show you my skills."

Even Garrett laughed at that.

A knock on the kitchen door preceded her mom by two seconds. Her short steel-gray hair stuck up in various appropriate directions as though she'd just stepped out of the stylist's chair. Which she had. Evette had owned her own salon for as long as Jayden could remember. She hugged the boys and went to the cabinet to find a bowl.

"I'll take the kids to school this morning and get them in the afternoon. I've got to run to town early then give Helen a perm." At sixty-three, her mother seemed much younger.

"Thanks, I need to get to the clinic."

The brothers brought their dishes to the sink, and Jayden rinsed them and stuck them in the dishwasher. Garrett went back to the table to eat his apple while Elliot dug in his backpack, asking, "When's Mr. Eric coming home?"

Her mother paused with a spoonful of oatmeal inches from her lips, but the spoon Jayden held clattered to the floor, splattering bits of oatmeal on the tile. She peered through the window above the sink at the darkened windows of the guest house across the field.

"They'll hear it at school," her mother said in a low voice. "Do you want me to do it?"

Jayden shook her head. Eric had been renting for nearly a year before Caitland and Robert had been killed. The boys knew him well. Three deaths in less than two months was far too much for a kid to deal with.

She slid a chair next to Garrett at the table then hauled another closer for Elliot. The older boy recognized bad news was coming. She could tell by his slumped posture and his reluctance to sit.

"We think Eric's been hurt and he may not be back." Elliot stood again and Garrett's eyes instantly filled with water.

"Did he go to be an angel in the clouds, too?" A tear trickled down Garrett's cheek, and Jayden wanted to throw up.

"We don't know for certain yet, but it looks that way. I want you to know what happened in case you hear about it at school." She swallowed the choking sob clogging her throat.

"Did he have a car wreck?"

She glanced at her mom who gave a slight nod. If Jayden didn't tell them the truth now, they'd probably hear part of it or even an exaggerated version later today.

"It wasn't a car wreck. We believe somebody hurt Eric and he might have died. We don't know for sure who, but the sheriff will find out."

"Why would somebody hurt Mr. Eric?" Garrett rubbed his face. She pulled her chair next to his so she could hold him close.

"We don't know."

"It was because of that stuff he was writing on the Loyalist people, wasn't it?" Elliot's eyes held a hint of anger.

"I said we don't know who did it or why, Elliot."

"*I* know. They're mean. They're the ones that call

us half-breeds. Eric said they didn't like him asking questions about their Militia group. He had a dog when he first came, but they killed it. Last year they painted mean stuff on the garage about me and Garrett. I'm going to get them one day, you wait and see."

His fist was in a knot, nearly as tight as the one in her stomach. "Elliot, no one knows who's responsible for hurting Eric. You're angry, very angry, and so am I. But we can't accuse people. It will only make more trouble."

She could see him processing the information. "We'll help the sheriff and the police if we can, won't we?"

She caught his hand in hers. "Of course we will."

"I've got to get my homework." Elliot's chair bumped the table as he wheeled around and left the room. Garrett pulled away and followed him.

"Poor kids can't catch a break," her mother said. "But do you think it's fair to only say he might be dead? They did find his watch on an arm."

"Until they've got DNA confirmation, we don't know Eric's dead."

Evette shook her head. "I think we know. And now when it's confirmed, you'll have to do this all over again."

Her mom was right. It wasn't likely that Eric was off enjoying himself somewhere while an appendage with his watch on it was buried near Cypress Landing. She twirled a napkin while her mother finished eating.

"Why didn't anyone tell me what was going on?"

Taking a sip of her coffee, Evette studied her. "What do you mean?"

"You know exactly what I'm saying. These idiots writing slurs on the garage and calling the kids names—why did Caitland and Robert stay? Why didn't they move when they adopted the kids? They should have known there'd be trouble when they tried to raise mixed-race children here."

Evette pushed the empty bowl away. "They stayed because this is their home and they didn't care what people said. The boys will have to confront those attitudes their whole life."

"But it's worse here because of that damn Militia. I can't believe they're still harassing people like that."

"What did you think when you left? It would go away?"

"No, but I thought the law would put those people in jail."

"They do put them in jail, then others take their place. And then they get out of jail anyway. But why am I telling you this? You were part of it. You understand how it works."

The air went out of Jayden as if she'd been punched. She expected comments like that now that she was home, just not from her own mother. "I was not part of that. I've told you a million times. I would never have been part of it." She squirmed in her chair. She didn't want to have this conversation again. It wouldn't change anything.

"That's not what I meant. Mark Dubois lived in it and you were his girlfriend."

"And because of that I'm as guilty of murder as he was."

"I didn't say that." Her mother patted her leg.

"No, I did, because I know how people in this town think."

"It doesn't matter now. These two boys need us, you and me. That's more important than people's theories."

"I guess I wasn't prepared to deal with the Militia and the past right now." Jayden went to the sink and clunked the last bowl in the dishwasher. "I better go to work."

Evette followed her. "None of us want to have trouble with the Militia. But we'll get by."

Jayden yelled for Kasey and the two of them hurried to her brother-in-law's old farm truck. The door creaked when she opened it but she didn't care. It was handy for taking to work, especially if she had to drive to someone's farm to treat a sick cow. Besides, it had belonged to Robert and she wanted to keep it for the boys.

JAYDEN PERUSED THE TABLE covered with plastic bottles, syringes and whatever else she could think of that might be needed to stitch a few cuts on a horse. She was waiting in the barn where they worked on large animals, which was attached by a breezeway to the main clinic. She could see Jeffrey Sabine at the rear door of the office talking on the cordless phone. He went into the building and she tapped her foot, fiddling with the disinfectant for the tenth time.

"He's on his way with the horse," Jeffrey said as he crossed the breezeway. "Says he has several bad cuts."

"How did he let his horse get cut?"

Jeffrey regarded her skeptically.

"Sorry," she added. "I don't mean to sound negative."

"Right, but you did and it would be better if you got rid of that attitude before he gets here. I didn't ask what happened. If I need to know I'll ask later."

He inspected the supplies. "Did you get the twitch?"

She groaned before starting for the storage room. Naturally, she'd forgotten something.

"Relax, Jayden. After you've worked with the big animals more you'll get used to them. I know you're used to working with dogs and cats, but I need you to do small and large here."

She placed the sticklike object with a chain on the end on the table. It resembled a torture device more than anything else. Of course, Jeffrey wouldn't use it unless he had to, if the horse wouldn't stand still. But Jayden hated it.

"Come on, J. What happens if I go on vacation and a client has an emergency with a horse or cow?"

"They could always use another vet."

"Oh, yeah, that's a great idea. A plus for business, don't you think?"

"You have to admit I'm getting better. It's only been a few weeks."

He grinned. "You're much improved. In the country you can't afford to be so specialized. That's the difference between Cypress Landing and Beverly Hills. You'll get used to it."

She gave Jeffrey an answering grin, even though she knew there were many bigger differences between Cypress Landing and Beverly Hills. He was right about one thing, she would adjust. She had to. When she'd arrived home after the accident, Jeffrey had been one of the first people to stop and see her. They'd been friends since grade school. He'd immediately offered her a job in his clinic if she decided to stay. Like she'd had a choice. Her mother had gawked at her as if she'd suggested moving to Mars when she'd wanted to move the whole family back to California. And Jayden couldn't make it without help. If she had to meet the challenge of raising two kids, she needed to do it where she had plenty of support, and that was here.

A truck, towing a horse trailer behind, roared into the drive.

"This will be a nice test for you." Jeffrey laughed as he hurried toward the vehicle.

She couldn't wait.

HE COULD SEE HER in the door of the barn. Luke knew when he left his house that Jayden Miller would be at the clinic. He remembered every detail from yesterday: her line of work, the color of her hair with the sun on it, the shine in those baby blues, that she was raising two kids, that she was Caitland's sister. The red stallion kicked the side of the trailer as Luke eased him backward. When his feet hit the ground, he danced sideways and half reared.

"I see Thor's happy to be here." Jeffrey smiled and gripped the halter when the horse finally settled all four feet on the ground. Luke grunted and the vet let go, so that he could lead the horse to the treatment area.

"What have you done to this animal?" Jayden demanded.

He looked at her standing in the entryway of the building and wished he didn't feel that twinge in his midsection simply because she was there. His horse had three cuts that would definitely need stitches. But for her to assume he was at fault made his skin itch.

"I didn't do this to him. He managed to figure out the new lock on the gate and took off early this morning. He got into a neighbor's barbed-wire fence."

She glared at him, and he felt guilty, as if he should have known the horse could open the gate, even though the guy at the farm store had promised him it was escape proof.

"He's underweight, too. Aren't you feeding him?"

Luke glanced at Jeffrey, who grimaced at his partner's words. "Yeah, I'm feeding him." The horse skittered along, nearly bumping the barn door as Luke led him in. He caught the halter and put a steadying hand on the animal's neck, making low clucking noises in his throat until the horse was calm. He frowned at her. "Do you think we can save the interrogation until we get done?" he snapped.

She was definitely as attractive as he remembered. Thankfully, she had an attitude that would make her easy to resist. Right now he wanted to get away as quickly as possible and maybe find a new vet, even if it would mean a forty-five-minute drive. Jeffrey held a syringe, and Luke noted the grim look he gave Jayden. She seemed to struggle briefly for her composure and finally ignored them to focus on the horse.

Jeffrey examined the cuts. "He definitely needs stitching together." But when he began cleaning the first wound, the horse snorted and plunged to the side, hitting Jayden with his shoulder. She stumbled and went to one knee. Luke reached to help her, but she waved him away.

"Hang on to the horse."

Across from him, he saw Jeffrey take hold of the twitch.

"No!" He and Jayden said it at the same time. Jayden scrambled to her feet.

"Let me get him settled." Luke glanced at her then he rubbed the horse's head.

The two vets waited as he rubbed Thor's ears, talking to him in a low voice. For several minutes no one moved, then the stallion sighed audibly, and Luke motioned for Jeffrey to begin. He heard Jayden mumble "horse whisperer" and he winked at her. She came closer and stroked the animal's neck.

"What's his name?"

The horse flinched as Jeffrey went to work on him and Luke made a soft grunting noise near his ear.

"Thor."

She touched the dark red coat. "God of law and order, champion of the people. Not a name I'd have expected you to choose."

He tried not to wince. Normally, Luke didn't care what people, especially a woman, thought of him. But something about her bothered him, maybe even touched him. He couldn't afford to think like that.

"I didn't name him. He was found by the humane society. I took him in."

"So you're a horse rehabilitator and defender of scum. Those two don't seem to go together."

"Jayden!" Jeffrey groaned. "Sorry, Luke. Jayden's had a tough month. She's on edge."

She stared at the floor after Jeffrey's reprimand. As rude as she'd been to him, Luke felt bad for her. Maybe it was because she was so perceptive. Of course he'd named the horse himself.

"Don't worry, Jeffrey. I don't mind Ms. Miller. We met yesterday and I'm more than happy to hear her opinions."

She gaped at him. He didn't plan on smiling at her, but he did. And he certainly hadn't expected to see her smile back at him. For the next few minutes while Jeffrey finished closing the cuts they remained on each side of Thor's head, stroking him.

"All right, I'm finished and Thor was great."

Luke ripped his attention from Jayden back to Thor. "Bill me, will you. I'm off to find a new lock for my gate."

He led the horse to the trailer and loaded him. Jeffrey and Jayden were still standing at the barn door when he got in his truck. Even with his back to them he could feel her watching him. He tried to convince himself it was his training that made him so perceptive of her.

## CHAPTER THREE

THE OUTBOARD MOTOR reverberated through the night air, and he wondered if the entire world could hear it. He always wondered that, but no one ever seemed to notice him. Luke steered toward the opposite side of the Mississippi. When the bank came into sight he slowed and nosed the boat into a tributary that emptied into the river. He went upstream a few hundred feet to a sandy spot then bumped ashore and tied off to a nearby tree. He didn't bother with a flashlight. He didn't need light to get where he was going. He preferred it to be darker—in fact, he wished there were clouds to cover the moon's glow. After ten minutes, the path he was following opened into a clearing with a wooden shack in the middle. A thin stream of light shone from under the door. He climbed the steps and knocked. Hearing a low voice answer, he went inside, wishing it didn't feel so natural, so normal.

"Damned mess we got now."

Joseph Bergeron sat in a metal folding chair in the dim glow of the light bulb hanging from the ceiling, a red plastic cup on the card table in front of him within easy reach. He grabbed the cup and spit, his lower lip bulged slightly with freshly ground tobacco.

Luke dropped into the metal chair across from him and it gave a squeaky protest. "I told you to leave the reporter alone, that he wouldn't disappear so easily."

"You think I gave the okay for this? Hell, I'm not that stupid. I'd at least have gotten everything he had on us before I did away with him." Joseph rested his arms on the table. "And I would have known better than to get that idiot Duke Swayze to tend to business."

"He's a member of the Militia and he doesn't mind doing a piece of work. Why wouldn't you use him?"

"Come on, he's crazy as a Betsy bug. Look at what we've got now. They found how many bodies at his place?"

"Four." Luke tried to stay calm. The memory of that day made him sick, and also brought to mind that damned goddess of a vet, the woman he was doing his best to forget.

"Right, four. Now doesn't that make your job a lot harder?"

"Yeah, it does. But if you didn't tell him to do this, who did? I doubt he came up with the idea on his own."

Joseph watched him, and Luke met his stare without faltering. He'd had enough practice at this. Besides, the Militia trusted him.

"There are others who didn't want that reporter to get away from here with whatever he might have found. We're working on a big project with another Militia group. We don't need this kind of attention. We haven't brought you in on this yet." Joseph scrutinized him for several seconds. "Maybe later."

Luke dipped his head slightly in agreement. Okay, they didn't trust him that much. These things took time.

"Do you think you'll be able to get ole Duke off?" Joseph asked.

"I don't know. He's not much help, spouting off crazy stuff every time the police question him, but I'll do what I can."

Joseph tapped the table before getting to his feet. "We'll take care of things on our end. We like having you in the community helping us."

"Glad to do it. I only wish I could do more."

Joseph went to the door, cracked it open and checked outside.

"You're doing what we need right now." He glanced at Luke. "Give me five minutes then leave." The man closed the door and was gone.

Luke sank deeper into the chair. What kind of project were they planning? He had a hunch who they were working with, but he couldn't get deeper into the ring of secrecy that surrounded the Acadian Loyalists, not yet. The Militia made their base camp across the river from Cypress Landing. Their members were scattered around the area. Some were like him, businesspeople doing whatever job they could to aid the cause, but keeping their affiliation hidden. Others, such as Duke Swayze, were open with their zealous beliefs. The leadership had a use for each.

He stretched to switch off the light, letting his vision get accustomed to the dark. His watch gave an eerie glow, reading one in the morning. Ten minutes had passed and he had another meeting to make on the other side of town.

FIFTEEN BASEBALL PLAYERS, all about ten years old, fidgeted in front of him. When most kids were playing soccer or enjoying the first few months of school with absolutely no other activities, those truly dedicated to this sport started a new season. Luke hadn't been able to help pick the team a few days ago, but his coaching partner, Pete Fontenot, appeared to have done a nice job. They'd gotten several of the best players in the area. He knew because he'd coached both seasons for two years. The fact that his usual coaching partner was a sheriff's deputy had been a stroke of luck for him. Joseph Bergeron had been pleased when Luke and Pete had started coaching together...as soon as he stopped laughing. "You're good, Taylor, really good," the man had said. And he was, but he worked hard at being good. It kept him alive.

As Pete told them their practice and game schedule, Luke waited quietly beside him. Five of the boys on this team had been with them in the spring. At the rear of the group he spotted Elliot Casio. He was big for his age and Luke was glad to see him. After his parents died, the boy hadn't been sure if he and his little brother would stay in Cypress Landing. Elliot was a polite kid and bit of a star in the league, but Luke was positive he dealt with mean-spirited comments at school, especially from kids whose parents were deeply ingrained in the Militia. Elliot's parents had adopted him and his brother and their racial origin was mixed—white, black, American-Indian, Asian. But the Casios had been doing an excellent job raising them, and the community, at least the real community and not the Militia, never gave their race a second thought. They were the Casio kids, the end. Unfortunately he'd been assigned to the case of the drunken idiot, a Militia member, who'd caused the crash that killed Caitland and Robert. Luke would have loved to see him in jail for vehicular manslaughter, but the evidence that the guy had been drunk disappeared and there was no case to be won or lost. It wasn't his fault…but the kids' aunt obviously thought so.

He whipped his head around, looking toward the fence where the parents sat in lawn chairs waiting for practice to begin. He didn't breathe, then he took a gasp of air and let it go. Pete glanced at him in mid-sentence but kept talking. Sitting in a chair next to Pete's wife was the object of several recent late-night dreams, Elliot and Garrett Casio's aunt.

Pete finished his speech, and Luke realized it was time to start the practice. He made a mental note not to let Jayden Miller distract him as he instructed the boys on what positions they'd be playing.

A FEW HOURS LATER, Luke waited at the front of his sprawling single-story house. It was way more than he'd expected when he arrived in Cypress Landing. It wasn't a restored antebellum like a lot of the homes in the area, but its wide porch with huge columns and multiple French doors across the front made it a nice mix of old South and old Acadian. He passed money to the pizza-delivery boy and, with Pete's help, hauled the boxes to his patio, spreading them onto several tables he'd arranged poolside. The late sun still had plenty of summer heat left in it, and the boys were enjoying what would probably be their last swim of the year.

"So, this is tradition for you, huh?"

Jayden appeared beside him, dropping a piece of pizza onto her paper plate.

"I guess. We do it every season."

"A heated pool, too. The public-defender business must be booming—or were you an ambulance chaser before you came here?"

He glared at her. Nearly everyone in town knew this house had been repossessed by the bank because the owner had gone to jail on a drug conviction, which explained how he had acquired such a nice home.

"I defended a guy and got him off. He started a business selling solar panels. He came and put this system in to heat my pool for free."

She didn't respond immediately, but picked at her slice. General bedlam surrounded them, fifteen boys yelling over the pizza as their parents tried to talk loud enough to be heard. Gradually the noise faded to a low hum. He noted the dark circles under her sea-blue eyes.

"I'm being rude, aren't I?" she asked.

"Yes, you are, but I get that periodically."

She shook her head. "My mom would have a stroke if she knew I'd talked to you like that. She says what happened with my sister isn't your fault."

Luke grinned. "If you promise to be nice, I won't tell her."

"So you know my mother. I should have guessed. She makes it a point to meet everyone in town."

"And she comes to most of the games."

Jayden took a bite of pizza and chewed for a minute, washing it down with a drink of soda from the can she'd set on the table next to them. "I didn't think of that, but I should have."

"She also cuts my hair." He fingered the slight curl above his ear. "I'm due for a cut, too. I haven't been to her since before…" He stopped himself, not intending to lead the conversation to that topic.

She must have noticed the flash of panic on his face because her lips swept into a slight smile. "Since before the accident, it's okay. We don't shy away from discussing it, especially since we didn't feel like justice was done."

Swallowing the groan that rose in his throat, he wished for the millionth time he hadn't been assigned to represent the guy who'd caused the Casios' crash.

"Your sister and her husband were good people and I hated that it turned out like it did, but I had no control over what happened to the evidence."

"It's still kind of hard to stomach."

"I don't like it any better than you."

She eyed him skeptically, then turned her attention to her soda.

"I've heard rumors that you get a lot of people off using questionable tactics."

Luke didn't want to guess what gossip around town had fueled her anger with that statement. "I imagine a few people think that. I do my job and I do it well because I owe it to the client."

"No matter what they've done."

"I don't get to pick and choose."

"I guess not."

"Elliot and Garrett are good boys, and I wouldn't have done anything to hurt them, if I'd had a choice. I hope they know it. The sheriff's office should take better care of their evidence."

"You're right about that. And don't worry, the boys don't hold what happened against you."

"So you're the only one."

She shrugged. "Guess so."

They watched the kids playing back in the pool. For now he could forget his purpose here and enjoy being part of the community. He found himself thinking again that if his life were different, Cypress Landing would be the kind of place he'd want to stay, to marry, to raise a family. Too bad his life wouldn't ever be like that.

"So, my mom cuts your hair." Jayden studied him as she tapped her empty plate.

"Yep, I met her a week after I moved here, and she informed me I needed a haircut and told me to be at her place at four that afternoon. I've been going ever since."

Jayden laughed aloud. A sound that made his body hum.

"Leave it to her to get the business of a good-looking man when he comes to town."

Luke's grin widened. Did she realize what she'd said?

"So you think I'm good-looking, huh?"

No, she hadn't realized, until now. She colored a light shade of pink and her eyes darted downward, refusing to meet his.

"I've got to throw this away." Nearly stumbling in her haste to leave, she tossed the paper plate in the garbage then hurriedly pulled an empty chair next to Leigh Fontenot. Jayden Miller thought he was good-looking. He tried not to puff out his chest and grin as he sauntered to the edge of the pool to join Pete.

"What do you think of Elliot's coach?" Leigh Fontenot tilted her head expectantly toward Jayden, awaiting her reply.

"You know I like Pete. I told you that when you first dated him and when he proposed, and when I came home for your wedding, and fifty other times."

Jayden ignored Leigh and tried to get comfortable in the lawn chair, but knew she never would. Not because the chair was too firm, but because she wanted to melt into the concrete beneath her feet. She'd admitted to a man she fully intended to dislike, that she thought he was attractive. A fact he'd probably heard from most of the women he'd come in contact with. Since he was Elliot's coach, she couldn't completely dislike him, but she had no business getting silly over him.

"Jayden." Fingers snapped in front of her. "I'm talking to you, okay?"

She focused on Leigh. "I'm listening."

"What did I say?"

"Fine, I wasn't listening, but I am now."

Her friend laughed. "Don't worry. Luke has that effect on most women, maybe all women. And he's the coach I wanted your opinion of, not Pete. But I'm sure you knew that."

Jayden squirmed again, sliding lower in the chair. "I don't have an opinion of him. I just met him, except of course he makes his living setting criminals free. I don't know how Pete can coach with him."

Leigh feigned shock. "And here I thought he was responsible for defending people who couldn't afford to pay for their own council."

"Well that, too, but don't forget he's the one who let Caitland and Robert's killer go." Jayden couldn't let that rest, not yet.

"Come on, Jayden, it wasn't like that. After the police report and lab work went missing, there was no case."

"And I'm to believe he didn't have anything to do with those things mysteriously disappearing."

"Of course he didn't. Luke's a nice guy. He and Pete have agreed to disagree on a few cases, but in the end, he's only doing his job."

"And what a paycheck he must be getting to

afford this place, the pool, the property, the barn." Jayden swung her arm, indicating their surroundings.

Leigh made a face. "Remember, this is your nephew's baseball coach we're discussing. Besides, this house had been repossessed by the bank because the guy who owned it went to jail for drugs. Luke happened along at the right time to buy it, cheap."

Jayden murmured, unconvinced. She wanted Leigh to stop defending him. As long as she could continue to dislike him, and continue to hold him responsible for the injustice of her sister's killer being set free, she could ignore the rush of excitement she felt every time she saw him. Luke had way too much sex appeal. Through half-closed eyes she studied him while he laughed with Pete and the boys by the pool. What she honestly meant was that he had way too much sex appeal to ever be interested in her. This was a man she couldn't trust, but she also couldn't deny being attracted to him. Guys like Luke went for women with perfect makeup and stylishly clipped hair, probably even big hair. One of the single moms in tight-fitting shorts and an even tighter tank top joined the men, her hand sliding along Luke's bicep as she talked. Luke listened attentively, and Jayden sighed. Yep, big hair and even bigger...

"She never quits. See that, Jayden?"

Glancing at Leigh, she pretended not to know what her friend meant. "See what?"

"Karen Singley has been chasing Luke since the day he came to Cypress Landing. You'd think she'd get the message. If he hasn't asked her out in two years, well, he ain't gonna."

Jayden smothered a giggle. "I guess I can depend on you to let me know if I'm ever making a fool of myself over a man, Leigh."

"Of course I will. Not that I'll ever have to. You aren't the type to do that, at least not anymore. I guess that one time you learned your lesson."

Jayden clutched the side of the chair. She concentrated on the other end of the pool, this time not seeing Luke or Pete. Leigh touched her hand, but she had to ignore her for a moment longer, had to nail the lid on the nightmares that surrounded her last months in this town years ago.

"I'm sorry, Jaybird."

Jayden nodded. She might have gotten angry if the comment had come from someone else, but not from Leigh, who'd been her constant support through their teenage years.

"I'm expecting uncomfortable moments now that I'm at the scene of the crime."

"You don't expect your best friend to trigger them. And there was no crime, either. No one thinks that."

"Everyone thinks that, but I know what you meant and you're right. I've learned plenty of lessons."

Leigh gazed past her, eyebrows arching. "Here's one lesson you won't want to miss." She inclined her head, and Jayden turned to see Pete and Luke stripping off their shirts to leap in the pool with the kids.

"I'll tell you, my Pete is a looker—and he's the

only man I'm interested in—but Luke's awesome, don't you think?"

That was the understatement of the century. Pete was muscularly slim, like a model you might see in a men's magazine. Luke's body was much thicker, though not bulky, and tanned to perfection. She imagined his bare chest had captured the attention of every female here, but she couldn't stop ogling him long enough to verify that. He tossed a water gun to one of the boys, then went under. When he surfaced, rivulets of water streamed down his face and he thrust the wet hair away from his forehead. His gaze locked with hers, and she felt herself blushing like a teenager. She hoped it was the sun. A slow smile curved his lips and he winked at her. A foam ball flew through the air, hitting him above the ear and he spun to attack the offender.

"Jayden, he winked at you. Did I miss something in the last few days?"

She still couldn't stop contemplating the spot where he'd been and she racked her brain for a cure to calm her galloping heart. "No, he's being ridiculous because I'm not fawning over him like I imagine half the women in town are."

"He's gone from that spot, in case you hadn't noticed." Her friend wore a wide grin. "You're right. The single women, and a few married ones, are on the prowl for him. But Luke has never been ridiculous and he's damned sure never winked at a female during one of his pool parties."

Jayden poked Leigh's leg. "Don't get matchmaking ideas. I could never be with a man I don't respect and I don't have a high opinion of a guy who's going to work hard to put Duke Swayze back on the street after he killed Eric Walsh."

Her friend let loose a slow breath. "It is kind of difficult to get past the idea of him doing that, even though it's what he's paid to do. He doesn't get to pick his clients. But the idea of Swayze killing Eric and getting off makes me sick to my stomach. Are they certain it was Eric's body?"

"They did find his watch on one of the bodies."

Leigh shivered. "That's gruesome."

Jayden stretched her legs and tried to relax. "Let's change the subject, okay? Tell me what's been happening in Cypress Landing for the past ten years or so."

Leigh snorted and launched into an account of their high school classmates, while Jayden made the appropriate replies. Raising the boys and rebuilding her life here were of vital importance to her. People in town would expect her to make mistakes, to fail, but she wouldn't. She watched her two little men bouncing in the water. They were good kids. She couldn't mess up, not this time.

# CHAPTER FOUR

THE TWO-BEDROOM HOUSE Eric had been renting was a stone's throw from her home. Jayden could remember when she'd been a teenager, a young couple bought this property and built the big house and the smaller one with it. They'd intended for the woman's mother to stay near them when she got older, but the couple had relocated long before that. The property was next door to her aunt, so her sister and Robert bought the place the minute it became available. Now Jayden lived there. It was the boys' home. The smaller house had become a source of extra income when her sister rented it, a simple act that had eventually led to an enormous problem for Jayden.

Things at the clinic had been slow, so when the sheriff's investigator called and wanted to search the place, she came in person to unlock it. The sheriff's car, a city police car and a van from the state crime lab sat in the drive. Jayden waited on the porch, unwilling to watch them trash the interior as they rummaged for evidence. She couldn't imagine what clues they hoped to find. Certainly Eric wasn't killed here, or at least she prayed not. The thought of that would keep her awake at night.

She rocked back and forth in the hanging swing on the tiny porch. The front door opened and the sheriff's investigator joined her. Unlike most of the sheriff's force, Jackson Cooper hadn't grown up in Cypress Landing. He'd taken the investigator's job and married a hometown girl not long before Jayden left, so she didn't know him that well. He was a huge man and a little scary. As he walked straight for her it was obvious he intended to sit with her. She squeezed to one side and prayed the swing's chains would hold both of them.

He eased against the slats. "Have you been in the house since Eric went missing?"

"No, I was waiting to see if his family might come for his things. And I knew you guys would be around."

"Have you seen anyone go inside? Anything suspicious…noises over here at night?"

She tilted her head, trying to see his face. "What are you asking, Officer Cooper?"

"I think an intruder's been in the house already. They didn't tear it apart, but a few things seem strange. There's no computer. Didn't he work on a computer?"

"Yeah, he had a laptop. But maybe it was with him."

"Could be, but we're not seeing notes or any sign of research. His kitchen and bathroom are so perfectly straight, they could be ready for a photo shoot."

"Eric was so messy. I find it hard to believe he'd straightened the place."

"Then I'm probably right. We're not the only ones who've been searching the place."

"What would anyone else want?"

"Same as us, detailed information on the story Eric was working on. Did he ever mention his work, tell you what he'd found?"

She groaned inwardly. Not this again. "He was doing an exposé on the Militia."

"The Acadian Loyalists, I knew that."

Her fingers tightened on the swing's chain. "What a joke. That's a significant historical name for the Acadian people. But this group has nothing to do with history, though they might like to think they do."

"So did you and Eric ever discuss the Militia?"

Past her house, through the trees, she could see her mother's house. A truck was parked in front of her beauty shop. Jayden rubbed her thumb over a rough spot on one of the wooden slats.

"Not much. He asked a few questions, since I'd grown up here…but I've been gone a long time. He never mentioned finding anything important. Do you think they're involved in his death?"

"Maybe. What do you think?"

"I think Duke Swayze is a psychopath and he's openly proud of his membership in the Loyalists."

She didn't look at Jackson, but out of the corner of her eye she could see his head turning as he inspected the area.

"We might want to question the boys. They've been around Eric."

"No. They've dealt with enough lately."

"But they might have heard or seen something."

Jayden shoved the swing backward as she got to her feet. "I said no. If they mention the least thing to me I'll call you, but I won't have them questioned by the police. They've lost their parents and now this with Eric. It's too much."

She tossed the keys to the house at him. "You can lock it when you're done. Leave the keys with my mother."

The wooden steps echoed with her footfalls as she stomped off the porch. Scrambling into the battered truck, Jayden tried to suppress her anger, which had begun to feel more like panic. She just wanted her life to be simple again, but she didn't see that happening any time soon.

As much as she'd hoped to forget about Eric and the Militia for the rest of the day, the clinic had remained slow and she'd hidden away in her office to try to distract herself with computer work.

At a tap on her office door, Jayden looked up from her computer to see a familiar face. She felt a rush of mixed feelings as the man held out his arms. Slowly she got to her feet.

"Mr. Arneaux—or am I supposed to call you General?" She came around her desk and stepped into his grasp.

"Mister is fine. I retired from the army."

"I heard."

"It's good to have you home, Jayden."

He released her and she sat in a small wooden

chair and positioned another one for him. "It's good to be home."

He sat and patted her knee. "Is it?"

She gave him a wry smile. "Not really, but I need to be here. California wasn't home anyway."

"You certainly stayed there long enough."

Her chest tightened so that her next words came out in a whisper. "Too many things here were hard to face."

He squeezed her leg with his large hand. "My son chose to be where he was, and what happened wasn't your fault. You have nothing to feel guilty about, Jayden."

She stared at the floor, a knot in her throat—what seemed like the millionth since she'd come home. "I still feel it, whether I should or not. Louis was a good friend. I don't think he knew Mark Dubois any better than I did. I know Louis didn't want to be in the army as you'd hoped, but he would have made a wonderful doctor." Her eyes burned and the tears she thought she'd finished crying years ago ran down her cheeks.

His hand on her knee tightened. "I'm sorry, too, but it happened and you weren't responsible. It was the Militia that caused his death."

When she looked up, he smiled. "That's enough tears. You have two nice young men to raise and you're going to do a good job. I came by to drop my dog off. I'll let you get back to work."

She stood with him and he gave her one more hug then left. Stumbling back into her chair, Jayden gripped the wooden arms. She was glad to have seen former General Reginald Louis Arneaux, but the memories that came with him weren't happy ones. His son had been best friends with her boyfriend, Mark. Now they were both dead.

## CHAPTER FIVE

JAYDEN PULLED INTO a parking spot shaded by the branches of an enormous oak. She sat waiting with the engine off as the light fall breeze fluttered the ends of her hair. In a few more seconds she'd be ready to go into the sheriff's office. The place brought back as many bad memories as General Arneaux but she had a responsibility to Eric and she needed to know more.

With a sigh, she got out of her truck and crossed the lot. The sun reflected off the metal trim on the door and she squinted in the bright light. She reached for the knob, just as the door opened.

A young man stepped aside with a smile and paused. Did she know him? His face seemed familiar, but she wasn't sure why. His dark hair was clipped close to his head but he ran his fingers through it as if it had once been longer and he'd forgotten it wasn't there anymore. His smile abruptly disappeared. But it was the look in his eyes that made her stomach churn.

"Hey, Kent. I kept digging and found that paper you needed. Good thing I caught you before you left." Sheriff Wright came out through the door

Jayden still held open. He glanced between the two of them as the younger man took the paper. "Jayden, you need to see me?"

"Yeah."

The young man Matt had called Kent turned away, half wadding the paper as he weaved his way through the parked cars.

"Who was that?"

"What?"

Jayden didn't realize she'd been whispering. She cleared her throat. "Who was that?"

"You don't remember him? I guess he's changed a lot over the past ten years. That's Kent Raynor."

She leaned against the edge of the door and closed her eyes.

"Oh, relax. It's been a long time, Jayden. Let's go to my office."

She followed behind Matt, wishing ten years could feel as long as it sounded and wondering how some things could change so much and others not at all.

Matt eased into his chair and kicked his feet up on the desk. "You're going to have to deal with people like Kent now that you're back."

"I was hoping he might have left."

"He did, but he's home now doing an internship while he's finishing law school."

"Great. He's a lawyer. He'll probably try to find a way to bring me to trial. He hates me."

Matt nodded. "Yep, he does. But that could change."

"If it hasn't changed in ten years, it's not likely going to."

"Ah, but you haven't been here for ten years to prove anyone's beliefs wrong."

"It's impossible to change the opinion of everyone."

Matt shrugged. "Maybe, but it doesn't hurt to try. I bet none of that is why you're here."

"You're right. I'd like to know the latest on Eric's case."

"Jayden, I can only tell you what we've already told the reporters. We're still trying to identify those bodies."

She rubbed her eyes. "Duke Swayze did this, Matt. I know it, and so do you."

"It doesn't matter what we know, only what we can prove."

She leaned forward in the chair. "What can I do? I want to help bring Eric's murderer to justice. He lived on my property, and I feel responsible."

Matt swung his feet to the floor. "You're a private citizen. There's nothing you can do but answer questions when we ask them and answer honestly. At the moment, we don't know Eric's dead, at least not conclusively."

Jayden stood, fists knotted at her side. "I wouldn't lie to the police, Matt."

"I don't want you to keep anything that could help the investigation to yourself so you can go off on your own private search. I know how you feel about the Militia and I know you're probably still angry. Don't try to get rid of it in the name of aiding Walsh's case."

She crossed her arms and didn't even try to deny Matt's statement. It was too close to the truth. "I want to work with you, not against you."

Matt came around the desk, closer to her. "I believe that. I also know you've got a stubborn streak, have had since you were a kid. I want you to stay safe."

She nodded and hurried to the door before he could see her watery eyes. "I'll check back if I think of anything."

She didn't wait for Matt's answer and didn't slow down until she was behind the wheel of her truck. She'd forgotten what it was like to have a community of people believe taking care of you was their job, even when they thought you'd done a terrible thing.

"THIS BACKPACK IS ALMOST bigger than you. Why don't you get another one?"

"Because I like this one," Garrett said.

Jayden tried not to groan. After her meeting with Matt at lunch, Jeffrey had left her in charge at the clinic so he could take care of family business out of town. She hadn't been thrilled to be left alone this soon. Naturally, after he'd been gone an hour, a farmer called, and she'd had to go help a cow give birth to what was expected to be a prize calf. Thankfully, she'd made the right calls and the cow and new calf were fine. But facing a situation she hadn't dealt with since vet school had left her too frazzled to fight with Garrett over a backpack.

"Put it on and wear it here in the aisle while I get paper towels. Then you can decide if you still want it."

She left the two boys and rounded the corner to

the next aisle, trying to keep the tiny shopping cart with one bad wheel from veering into the shelves. The errant cart jerked to the right and bumped the hip of a girl with blond curls hanging down her back.

"Sorry." Jayden whipped the cart on course, trying not to stare, but the profile of the girl tickled a memory for her. She'd know Amy Dubois anywhere. She dug her fingers into the plastic of the eight pack of paper towels and tossed it in her cart. The cart skittered to the side as she tried to push away without looking back.

"I know it's you, Jayden Miller, even if you don't say a word to me. I heard you were back, and you haven't changed a bit."

Jayden tried not to chew her lip as she turned around. "Hi, Amy."

The blonde snorted. "I knew you recognized me."

She caught herself unconsciously wiping her sweaty palms on her jeans. "You've changed— grown up a lot—but I could still see it was you. I didn't figure you'd have anything to say to me."

The other girl took a step toward her. "Oh, I've got plenty to say to you. But this isn't the time."

"Aunt J., your idea worked. After Garrett saw the backpack was gonna bang him in the back of the knees all day, he picked a different one. He—" Elliot's voice tapered off as he looked between his aunt and the woman in front of her.

Jayden glanced at him and smiled, though her lips felt tight. "That's good. Run back and stay with him. He shouldn't be alone in the store."

Elliot trotted to the end of the aisle then made the corner.

Amy shook her head. "I heard you were raising your sister's kids. Crazy, huh? Wonder what my brother would have to say about that?"

Jayden had asked herself that question before and still didn't have an answer. She'd always imagined she and Mark held the same beliefs, but one horrible night had changed everything. Amy, she realized, was waiting for a reply.

"I don't know. I guess I never knew your brother, at least not like I thought I did."

"Yeah, and nobody knew you, either. My dad's not too happy you're back. No one is. So you better watch yourself and those kids, too. Be sure to stay clear of my family."

The girl's hip bumped the shopping cart again as she passed, but Jayden didn't turn to watch her go. She sagged against the shelf next to her. A thump in the next aisle caught her attention and she left the cart behind in a mad dash to check on the boys. A small pile of backpacks and an entire box of pens lay on the floor. Elliot stood in the middle of the mess, his fists tight and his face cherry-red. Garrett stared at his brother with saucer eyes.

"What's the matter, Elliot?" She knelt in front of him and could see his nostrils flaring, but he didn't answer.

"That big, mean man said something to him," Garrett volunteered.

"What man?"

"He just left."

She raced to the front of the store and peered through the large windows. In the parking lot, Amy stood by a huge new dual-wheel truck. The man beside her had a grip on her arm and was nearly lifting her off the ground. He released her suddenly and walked to the driver's side of the vehicle while Amy crawled into the passenger's seat. Jayden knew the man's face, but not his name. It didn't matter. He was Militia. That was enough to know.

Back in the school-supply aisle, Elliot had calmed down and was on his knees gathering pens and placing them back, while his brother stacked the backpacks.

"What did the man say to you, Elliot?"

The boy shook his head.

"You can tell me. It'll be okay."

He dropped the last pen in the box before looking up at her. "It doesn't matter what he said and it won't ever be okay."

She knelt and hugged him. "You're right. It won't ever be okay for anyone to not be nice to you, because you're a good person and that's all that matters. There are people in this world who are simply narrow-minded. Do you know what that means?"

"Yeah, stupid."

She smiled. "Good enough. Now, what if we go to Ray's Fish House to eat?"

Elliot brightened. "Really?"

"Yes, is that strange?"

"Mom didn't like us to eat out during the week, only on special occasions."

"Well, we're buying Garrett this backpack, and I think that's a special occasion, don't you?"

"Oh, yeah, a new backpack is super-special."

"Can I get shrimp and frog legs?" Garrett asked, pulling her toward the front of the store.

Both boys bounced up and down while she paid, and she wondered if they might run to the restaurant rather than wait and ride in the car with her. On her way out the door she glanced at the empty parking spot where the white truck had been. Idiots, all of them, but now that she was here she might get the opportunity to put some Militia members in their place. The idea put a smile on her face.

She was still smiling when she slid into a seat at the family restaurant. She lifted her hand to wave at one of their neighbors then flipped through the menu, trying to decide what she wanted while she and Garrett waited for Elliot to return from the bathroom.

"Look who I found." Elliot made a running slide into the chair across from her and it wobbled onto two legs.

"Elliot, be careful!" Jayden half rose from her seat.

A hand gripped the boy's chair to keep it from toppling over. The deep blue eyes of Luke Taylor settled on her, and she felt her skin tingle. She nearly frowned but caught herself. She didn't want the boys to see her agitation.

"Coach was about to get an order to go, but I told him he should eat with us."

"If that's okay?" Luke towered above her and she wished she didn't like the sound of his voice quite so much.

She glanced at the boys, who were thoroughly excited at the idea of eating with the baseball coach.

"It's fine if you want to."

He nodded, still pinning her with a look she couldn't quite read. His eyes seemed to lighten and he smiled. Unable to stop, she smiled back. She could've kicked herself for giving in to his charm. His yellow shirt was rolled up at the sleeves and the collar was unbuttoned as if he'd recently pulled loose a tie. The shirt stretched across his chest when he moved, and he seemed to take over their table with his presence.

"Coach Taylor's a lawyer," Elliot announced as Luke settled into a chair.

"Yes, I know."

Elliot launched into a discussion of baseball, which he clearly deemed much more important than being a lawyer. Having his coach sit at the table and give him his undivided attention turned the boy into a chatterbox. Throughout their meal they discussed the teams they would play and whether or not they would do well against them. Not that she minded. It kept her from having to join in and also gave her plenty of time to study the man who made her angry and nervous at the same time. She wasn't oblivious to the interested looks they got from the other diners, either.

"We're through. Can we go play the games?"

Discouraged, Jayden glanced to the machines across the room. And she thought she'd get away without having a conversation with Luke. She nodded and began digging in her purse for coins, but before she could produce any Luke had pulled several dollars from his pocket.

"Let me, mine's easier to get to."

She dropped her purse between her feet and didn't argue. The boys raced away, and her stomach instantly tightened.

"Thanks for letting me eat with you."

She wiped her hands on a napkin. "The boys enjoyed it. They like you."

"Why do I feel like there's a lecture coming about being a role model and how if I get this Swayze guy off I won't be a good one?"

She didn't like it that he could already read her so well. "Let's not discuss your job right now."

Luke nodded. "So, we'll discuss something else."

"Right. How's your horse?"

He smiled. "Thor's fine, and hopefully I've gotten a latch on the gate he can't get open."

"That's good."

She fell silent and wondered what to say next.

"How's being home compared to…where you were?"

She turned back to Luke. "Very different. I was working in Beverly Hills the past two years."

"I guess this was a change. Vet to the stars, huh?"

"Actually, we were."

He paused with the glass of iced tea halfway to his mouth. "You're joking."

"Nope. More than half of our clients were in the film or music industry, and quite a few were famous."

"No cows and horses for you to deal with there."

"That's right, and I don't mind telling you it's been an adjustment."

Luke focused his attention on Garrett and Elliot for a few seconds and she studied his profile, the way his lashes curled long and thick and his lips were smooth and not too full.

He faced her, and she tried to look away but she knew he'd caught her staring.

"I'll bet the job hasn't been the only difficult situation since you've been back."

She pushed away the remnants of the fried catfish she couldn't eat. "It's been very hard, but they're special kids. I hadn't expected to be a parent this soon, though."

"You could have let someone else do the job or sent the boys back to foster care."

"Don't think it didn't cross my mind." She stopped short and took a drink of her tea then wiped her mouth with the napkin. "I can't believe I said that out loud. And to you. A person I barely know."

He reached out to stop her from shredding the napkin she held. His grip was firm and warm and didn't make her uncomfortable as she would have imagined.

"Anyone would have thought that. Two boys are a big responsibility. You had to uproot yourself and leave behind your friends and your job. If it hadn't crossed your mind, I'd be surprised."

"My sister has had Elliot and Garrett since they were babies. They couldn't go anywhere else. Besides, if they'd been her birth children instead of adopted, I wonder if I'd have had such a thought. Anyway, they're as much hers as if she'd delivered them herself, so that makes them family and mine to raise."

"They seem to be adjusting well."

She twisted so she could see the boys playing. "It gets a little better every day. They'll be fine."

They sat quietly, while the two boys remained across the room. She wondered what Luke might be thinking.

"Has anyone assigned you a day to be dugout mom?"

The change of subject surprised her. "I'd say no, since I don't know what a dugout mom is."

"All the parents get assigned a game to bring water and sports drinks for the dugout. You sit in with the boys during the game. It helps keep them in order while we're on the field coaching. You know, make sure they're ready for their turn at bat, that kind of thing."

"Oh, okay. I can do that. Where do I sign up?"

"I'll have Leigh Fontenot call you. She makes the list."

Jayden became conscious of Luke's hand still covering hers, his thumb making a path back and forth on her skin. She was mesmerized by its motion and when it stopped she found Luke watching her, his eyes almost violet. He trailed his fingertips over her palm then glanced across the room and waved.

She turned to see who'd caught his attention and stiffened.

"Kent Raynor." Jayden bit her lip, not sure if she'd said the name aloud.

Luke's hand had covered hers again. "He works for me. It's an internship he's doing for school."

Obviously she had said the name aloud. "I heard he was studying to be a lawyer. I'd never have expected it."

"Why not?" he asked. She pushed her napkin around on the table with her free hand as she avoided answering him. "Jayden, I'd like you to answer that question since he's working in my office. If you know a terrible secret about him, I'd like to be in on it."

She took an unexpectedly shaky breath. Terrible memories, but they weren't secret. Luke simply didn't know. "No, I've never known him to do anything wrong. Kent had it tough when he was young, that's all. His father was very hard on him and his mom. Then his dad was killed by the police in a raid to break up an illegal weapons ring. It was a big story in town. I'm sure you've heard of it, even though it was a long time ago."

"I know about that. Kent seems to be fine, though."

She nodded. "I'm sure he is."

Luke gave her hand a final squeeze and stood. "I better go. I enjoyed the meal, and the conversation."

He left and Jayden rubbed her skin, still warm from his touch. The table rocked slightly as the boys dropped into their seats.

"Are we ready to go?" Elliot asked.

She nodded, closing and opening her hand. What was wrong with her? At the cash register she discovered that Luke had already paid for their meal and she wanted to kick herself for not being more attentive so she could have stopped him.

They were nearly home when the boys' brought up Luke.

"Coach Taylor is nice. I like him, don't you?"

Jayden tried to see Elliot's face in the rearview mirror, but it was too dark. "Yeah, he seems like a good coach."

"I'm glad he stayed to eat with us."

She didn't respond because she wasn't sure if he expected an answer and she really wasn't sure if she was glad she'd eaten with Luke.

"Do you think he could eat with us again, maybe at our house?"

Jayden glanced in the mirror again. "I don't know why he'd do that, Elliot."

"If you invited him, he would."

"We don't have a reason to invite Mr. Taylor to eat with us."

"But you were holding hands." Ah. Garrett had suddenly decided to get to the point. As much as she'd liked the feel of Luke's hand on hers, she wished it hadn't happened. The boys didn't need to get any weird ideas.

"He was making a point, not holding my hand."

She turned into their drive and parked the car. Garrett leaned over the front seat. "What does that mean?"

"We were talking, and he wanted to be sure I understood what he was saying so he put his hand on mine. Grown-ups do that occasionally."

The boy flopped backward and opened the door.

"Looked like hand-holding to me," she heard him muttering as he jumped to the ground.

## CHAPTER SIX

LUKE THUMBED THROUGH the money in the envelope and nodded at the man across the desk. They didn't carry on a conversation because this guy wasn't sent here to talk. Just to deliver. Generally, Luke wouldn't have allowed one of the Militia to waltz into his office, but when he was defending one of their own, having them here wasn't a big deal. People would have thought it odd if the Militia *didn't* show up to check on their brothers.

His phone buzzed and he picked it up. A smile shot across his face before he realized it, and he quickly forced a frown. Jayden Miller was waiting in the other room at his secretary's desk.

"That's it then," Luke said. "Tell our friend I appreciate his help and I'm doing all I can."

"He knows."

Luke went to the door and the other man followed, leaving without another word.

Jayden sat in one of the wooden chairs watching his visitor until he disappeared down the hall. Luke motioned twice for her to come in before she got up. Her hair was pulled back and she wore faded green scrubs. When she passed he noticed the slight scent of disinfectant. Why his pulse slammed into high gear at the sight of her he had no idea. As one of the few eligible bachelors in town, he'd had numerous women walk through his door wearing fairly provocative attire and smelling like they'd stepped from a scented bath. He wasn't sure what it said about him that scrubs and the smell of wet dog and disinfectant turned him on.

"Jayden, what can I do for you?"

She'd walked over to the window and stood staring out at what he knew was a lovely view of the county jail's fenced yard. She didn't seem bothered by it and didn't answer immediately. Moving next to her, he tried to see what had caught her attention. Ah, Duke Swayze smoking a cigarette in the yard.

She turned away suddenly. "I want to know if you've found out any more about Eric Walsh."

He should have known that was what she'd want.

"Jayden, I couldn't tell you anything even if I had found new information, which I haven't. Unfortunately, this client isn't the most cooperative one I've ever had."

"That's because he's nuts."

"I agree with you, and we'll probably plead insanity."

"What!"

"You heard me."

"That's ridiculous. Swayze needs to pay for what he's done."

"If he's mentally ill, like you say he is, don't you think he needs treatment?"

"He simply doesn't care. He can hurt people and not feel bad about it—and he knows exactly what he's doing."

Luke sighed again. "Jayden, it's my job to do the best I can for him. I'd rather not argue with you. It is what it is."

"I'm not arguing about your job. I feel responsible for what happened to the man renting a house from me and I want to see his killer brought to justice. Is that so wrong?"

He reached for her, but she jerked away. He didn't even know why he'd made the attempt. They certainly didn't have enough of a friendship for him to comfort her, but he very much wanted to get closer to her. He rubbed the back of his neck instead.

"It's not wrong to want that, but I can't help you get the answers right now."

Jayden went back to the window. She needed Luke to give her information, but she didn't want to need anything from him. "Eric was on to something with the Militia. He never said what, but he was excited. I think Swayze knows."

Luke shoved the sleeves of his shirt farther up. "He may know, but he's not talking to me or anyone else that I know of. He says he didn't kill any of those people. He told me the Militia has been using his property as a body dump for years and now they want him to take the fall for it."

She glanced at him then crossed to the door, her

rubber-soled shoes slapping against the wooden floor. "So that's the angle you're using. If you get Duke Swayze off you'll be setting a murderer free. How will you feel when he kills the next person? What will you say to the family?"

"Jayden, if the evidence is there then the jury will find him guilty no matter what I do. If it's not there, he may go free because we try not to put people in jail when there's no evidence to prove they committed the crime. It's called the justice system."

"Like with my sister and her husband, huh?" The words leapt from her before she could stop them. She'd made up her mind the other day to stop making herself sick because the man who caused Caitland and Robert's deaths had gotten off. Not even her mother held Luke responsible for that, but she couldn't seem to let it go. Luke's shoulders sank slightly and he rubbed his palm across his forehead without meeting her eyes.

She wasn't helping anyone by attacking him all the time. "I'm sorry. I don't mean to keep beating you up about it."

"Sure you do," he said with a wry smile. "You want somebody to pay. I'm the most likely target."

It was her turn to stare at the floor. "You're right. I do want to see justice for Caitland and Robert, but I shouldn't hold this against you."

He stuck his hands in his pants pockets. "Whatever you need to do to get through this, I understand."

She shook her head. "Treating you unfairly isn't

going to help me feel better. Right now I can't think of anything that would."

He took a step toward her, stopping when she reached for the doorknob. Jayden paused. Having someone strong and capable hold her and tell her she could do this—raise these kids, make a life here— would help tremendously. But she couldn't say that to a man she still thought she should dislike. Didn't he have at least some responsibility for what happened? The only thing she knew for sure was that she was attracted to him beyond good sense. Jayden hated herself for the way she couldn't stop staring at Luke's muscled forearms below the rolled-up sleeves of his neatly pressed shirt, or for noticing how his blue eyes darkened to storm clouds when he was angry or frustrated. She especially hated that, for a fleeting second, she wondered what color they'd be when he was passionately kissing someone, maybe even her.

Pulling her hand away from the door she pressed the heel of it against her forehead. "Could I get a soda? I'm thirsty."

"Sure. I'll have to run upstairs to the vending machine but I'll be right back."

"Thanks." She stepped aside to let him leave and was thankful that he was as nicely mannered as she'd expected. The instant the latch clicked behind him, Jayden scurried to Luke's desk and began thumbing through papers.

She hadn't come here to snoop. She only wanted to get a few details about Eric, to appease her conscience. When Luke's previous visitor strolled from his office, she'd tried to hide behind a magazine. His real name eluded her but his face and nickname were wedged in her memory. Why he was known as Speck she wasn't sure but he'd been a friend of Mark's family and a devotee of the Militia. What was he doing here? Did he have input into the Duke Swayze case or was the public defender taking on other Militia cases on the side? She was attracted to Luke and everyone in the parish seemed to believe he was an upstanding member of the community. If he was hiding something, she wanted to know.

Digging in his desk drawers was possibly a crime. When she opened the second one and saw the envelope full of cash, her throat closed and she struggled to breathe. What would he be doing with a wad of cash in his drawer? It was none of her business and could have been for anything, but it bothered her more than she wanted it to. With a shove she closed the drawer and went to lean against the wall near the door. She wanted to like Luke, even though she wasn't sure she could trust him. He could be in the Militia, which would be a dangerous thing for her and what was left of her family.

She heard Luke's footfall outside the door before it opened and he came in holding a soda.

"Thanks." She took the drink and started to leave.

"Don't you want to stay and drink that?"

Jayden shook her head. "I've bothered you enough today. I'll be going."

His brow furrowed and he glanced around the

office, making Jayden cringe and hope she didn't look as guilty as she felt.

She forced a smile. "I need to get back to the clinic. Jeffrey will be wondering why I've taken such a long lunch break."

Halfway through the door she paused. Luke confused her. So much about him shouted nice guy, but there was still that hint of mystery, of a man hiding a part of himself. "Be careful of the Militia, Luke. They're committed to their cause, very committed."

She could feel his eyes on her as she hurried through the door. Let him dwell on that. Maybe he'd appreciate that he was mixing with dangerous people. In the parking lot she paused in the middle of opening the truck door. Glancing up she saw Luke watching her from the window. What if he was one of those dangerous people? Could he fool everyone in town so completely?

LUKE TIGHTENED THE GIRTH of Thor's saddle one last time before pulling himself onto the horse's back. The animal pranced sideways, and Luke patted his neck until he calmed down. Pete's house was only a couple of miles from his if he followed the paths through the woods. This was their last free Saturday before the baseball games started. He made a few rounds in the open field to give Thor extra exercise then he turned in the direction of the Fontenots. Thor negotiated the path without much assistance from him, and Luke let himself replay Jayden's visit to his office a few days ago. She was difficult to read, and he didn't like that. Every time the subject of Duke Swayze came up, or the fact that Luke defended members of the Militia, Jayden's temper boiled. His work here was going well if a bit slower than he would have liked. He needed to move on before he got tied up in this place and its people.

The trees thinned and Thor trotted into Pete's backyard. The deputy waved from the patio where he sat across from his nephew, Steven Owens. Leigh's sister was a single mom who couldn't seem to get herself together, so she flitted from one job to another and one boyfriend to another. Her ten-year-old son spent most of his time with his aunt and uncle, thus explaining Pete's interest in coaching. People usually thought Luke simply loved kids and baseball since he had no other reason to coach, or at least no reason they knew, which was exactly the image he'd intended to create.

He unsaddled Thor and slipped a halter on the horse's head in place of the bridle and let him loose in the paddock with Steven's horse before crossing the yard.

"Hey, Coach."

"Hi, Steven. Have you two already got the season planned?"

"Almost," Pete answered.

"Elliot and his aunt will be here soon and he can help us, too."

Luke lowered his eyebrows, but Pete only shrugged and said, "Steven, go help Leigh with the dinner. She's already run me out of the kitchen."

The boy left and Pete pointed to a chair. Luke dropped into it, completely unsure of how he was feeling now that he knew Jayden could show up any minute.

"Don't blame me. It was Leigh's idea to cook a big meal and invite Jayden when she found out you were coming. She's got matchmaking on her mind and there's no stopping her."

Luke leaned back in the chair. "She does know that Jayden and I don't exactly get along very well, doesn't she?"

"She heard the two of you had dinner together recently."

"What?"

"You were spotted at Ray's Fish House the other night."

"That's ridiculous. I was going for takeout, but the boys saw me and wanted me to eat with them."

"Did you sit at a table with them and eat?"

"Yes."

"Was Jayden there?"

"Of course she was there."

"Then you had dinner together."

Luke groaned.

Pete tossed him a beer from the small cooler at his feet. "Don't worry. Leigh's determined that a man in Jayden's life will help her settle in here after all she's been through lately. If you aren't interested, she'll get the message eventually."

Luke groaned louder, and Pete grinned before

emptying his can and tossing it back in the cooler. At the sound of a car, he got up.

"That's probably Jayden now. Who knows, if my wife throws you together enough, the two of you may give up and start dating."

Luke stayed in his seat as Pete left to meet Jayden and the boys. He couldn't afford to date anyone, but Pete didn't know that. Anytime he'd felt the need for female companionship he'd been sure to leave Cypress Landing far behind to find it. He had to admit if things were different, he'd definitely be after Jayden. The sight of her rounding the corner rerouted his blood flow so that it left his brain and drained to…*other* parts of his body. Pete had told her he was here because she showed no surprise as she sank into a chair. The boys shouted a greeting as they raced past with Steven following, all three carrying baseball gloves. They stopped in the middle of the yard and started playing catch. Luke kept waiting for Pete, but he didn't appear. He tilted his head as if it would help him see around the house.

"He's not behind me. He's inside."

Luke turned to Jayden. "Why?"

"Leigh decided that he should stay and help her so you and I could talk."

"Oh."

One corner of her mouth turned up then her shoulders shook as she started laughing. "I see you're pleased."

"No, I didn't mean it like that. I know you don't want to be stuck with me."

"I'm not stuck with you. I could get up and go inside."

"So you want to sit out here with me?"

She colored slightly and he noticed her take a quick inventory of his body. Then she reddened even more as she obviously became aware of what she'd done. An emotion he couldn't begin to describe passed over her face then her features hardened. She moved forward in her chair so that she was only a foot from him.

"You're a good-looking man, I'll give you that. But there's something about you I don't like. Unfortunately, you're my nephew's baseball coach, and the boys—along with numerous other people—seem to like you. A lot. So I'm willing to be around you to make them happy."

Luke inched closer until his knees were nearly touching hers. Not exactly the smartest move he'd ever made. At this distance her fresh, flowery scent filled his nose with every breath he took and for a few seconds he forgot what he'd been about to say.

"It's a shame you have to sacrifice yourself for the good of everyone else." He put his hand on her knee and moved his thumb back and forth across her skin. "I'll do everything I can to make the time you're forced to spend with me as painless as possible."

He could see she was holding her breath and her eyes had widened, but he figured he was suffering the worst of it. His hand ached to stay where it was, maybe even explore farther. But he got to his feet and left her sitting there while he went to join the boys.

## CHAPTER SEVEN

THE USUAL CHAOS of the evening had settled into peace and quiet as the boys fell asleep. Smiling, Jayden closed Garrett's door and went to the kitchen to put away the last of the dishes. A car's headlights lit up the living room and she folded the dishrag, dropping it on the counter. She peered through the glass of the front door and shook her head.

Within minutes her mother had climbed the steps and whizzed into the house.

"Mom, you do know it's ten o'clock, don't you?"

"Of course I do. I've been out to dinner with friends."

"What place in Cypress Landing serves dinner this late?"

"I never said I was in Cypress Landing. The group of ladies going on the cruise went to dinner together. What's a single girl like you doing home on a Friday night?"

Jayden had forgotten about the cruise her mother would be taking soon. She sank into her favorite chair and hugged a pillow.

"In case it slipped your mind, I live here with two

children under the age of twelve, so I'm not likely to be out partying. Besides, the only friends I have here are married."

"I didn't mean partying. You should be on a date."

"With who? Good grief, I've only been here a short time. I haven't met any single men and, to be honest, I'm not looking. I've got all I can handle with the new job and the boys."

"I could help more. You have to let me."

"I don't need more help, and I especially don't need people matchmaking for me."

"Fine, I won't try to set you up with any of my clients."

She narrowed her eyes, then started to laugh. "Well, that's a relief, since the only men I've seen at your shop getting a haircut were all over sixty."

Evette walked past her chair and gave Jayden's foot a kick. "Don't knock the older men. You might like them. Now come in the kitchen and give me a piece of that dessert you made yesterday."

Jayden got to her feet. "I thought you ate out."

"I did, but I didn't get dessert and I've been driving for an hour."

She took the pan from the refrigerator and cut through the layers of whipped topping, chocolate, cream cheese and pecans then dumped the slice on a saucer. After a brief debate, she cut a piece for herself.

Sticking a forkful into her mouth, the older woman smiled and closed her eyes. "This stuff is so good."

Jayden sat down across from her at the kitchen table and nodded. "Yep, sweet on the lips, sticks to the hips."

"Oh, don't ruin it."

She laughed. "All right, we'll say it's calorie-free."

"That's better. I do have a male client who's not over sixty. As a matter of fact, he's only a bit older than you, and quite an eligible bachelor in town."

Her mother didn't have to say the name. Jayden remembered Luke saying Evette cut his hair.

She shook her head. "Not interested."

"You've got to be. Every single female for miles is."

"Well, I'm not."

Her mother was silent for a moment. "What's that for?" She nodded toward the back door. Jayden cringed. Explaining what she was doing with the cooler waiting at the back door would sound ridiculous after her last statement.

When she didn't answer her mother said, "Are you and the boys going somewhere tomorrow?"

She groaned in resignation.

"Luke Taylor wants to take the boys fishing out on Lake Sewell tomorrow. We're bringing drinks, sandwiches and chips."

Her mother put the last bite of dessert in her mouth and leaned back in her chair, chewing slowly. She swallowed and wiped her mouth.

"Let me get this straight. You're going to the lake tomorrow with a man you're not interested in."

"No, the boys are going fishing with Elliot's

baseball coach, who they think is the greatest man on earth right now. I'm not sure why."

"And you're going because—"

"I'm going because I don't know him well enough to trust him alone with the boys. I wouldn't have let them go, but he didn't ask me first, he asked them. Then what was I going to do? They were so excited, I couldn't tell them no."

"How is it that you don't trust the public defender for this parish, a highly respected man?"

"He rubs me the wrong way," Jayden countered.

Getting to her feet, Evette put her saucer in the sink then faced her daughter. "I think you're afraid he's going to rub you the right way and you're scared of it."

"That's ridiculous."

"Have you had one serious boyfriend since Mark was killed, since you left here?"

Jayden stared at the table. "I'm not interested in getting serious with a man."

"You're afraid you'll make a mistake again, use poor judgment with a man. But, Jayden, sometimes it happens—so what? Look at me. Your father was the wrong man, but I got you and your sister out of it so it wasn't all bad."

"And what do you think I got from Mark?"

"A lesson in what you're not looking for in a man." Her mother's hand closed over her shoulder. "One day you need to give someone else a chance. Maybe it won't be Luke, but someone."

"How can you say that when you've never remarried? You say I should be dating, but what about you?"

"I am dating."

Jayden's eyes widened, even though she tried to stop them. Her mother's hand immediately flew to her mouth as if she could recapture what had already escaped.

Her mother was dating and hadn't told her. That was strange. "So who's the mystery man because I sure haven't seen him?"

It was her mother's turn to squirm. Jayden would have felt sorry for her, but she knew this woman wouldn't give her a minute's peace if she thought Jayden had a secret boyfriend.

"Well?" she prompted when her mother still didn't answer.

Evette rolled her eyes and fussed with her hair. "All right, I have been meeting a man occasionally. We're driving to New Orleans tomorrow night for dinner and the theater."

"Why haven't you said anything?"

Her mother glanced at the floor. "I wasn't sure how you'd feel about it, or even what people here would say when we're seen together."

Jayden raised her eyebrows but didn't speak.

"It's Reginald Arneaux, Jayden."

Her mother was dating the father of Louis Arneaux. Louis—her friend who'd died in the explosion that some thought she'd helped set off.

"Is it okay?"

Jayden tried to shake her head clear. "Of course, that's fine, Mom." She hugged her. "He stopped by the clinic the other day."

"He doesn't hold you responsible for what happened. He believes you didn't know about the bombing."

"He's always said that."

Her mother nodded and walked to the front door. Jayden followed.

With one hand on the knob, her mother looked back. "Be nice to Luke tomorrow. He's a good guy, and you might find that you enjoy being rubbed the wrong way. I'd definitely let him rub me any way he wanted."

"Mother!"

"What? Anyone can see he's very sexy."

"I'm your daughter, remember? I don't think you're supposed to talk to me this way."

"Oh, come on. I've always been honest with you, and you're grown up. You can take it." With that she left, closing the door behind her.

Setting the lock, Jayden watched the car leave then turned off the lights to go to bed. Before she came here, she had gone out on Friday nights—to clubs or to dinner with friends. Things were different in Cypress Landing and she had expected that. She'd found that she didn't mind at all. The idea of having a husband, a family at home, crossed her mind frequently, even when she lived in California. She simply wasn't sure if she could pull it off. She'd failed in her first relationship so completely, a second one hadn't been worth the effort. Now she had the boys, and if they never had a father in the house, so what? There'd never been a father when she was growing up, and she'd turned out fine, hadn't she? Well, maybe not fine, but perfectly okay.

If Luke was mixed up with the Militia, she'd find out. Everyone here seemed to have the man on a pedestal. Unfortunately, she might have to knock him off.

"HOW MANY DOES THAT MAKE?" Elliot asked as Luke helped him get the fish off his hook and drop it into the live well.

"That's three apiece for you and Garrett, and one for me."

"None for Aunt J." Elliot looked at her reproachfully.

Luke nodded. "It helps if you actually put your hook in the water."

"Hey," she said, "I'm perfectly fine sitting here drinking my soda and watching you guys."

And she was. For the first few minutes of the fishing trip she had tried to fish, but she found relaxing in the cushioned seat of Luke's shiny bass boat much more enjoyable. Stretching out, she'd forgotten about everything except the sun and the cool breeze. When she saw Luke like this, helping the kids fish, and saw how the boys loved being around him, it was hard to imagine him being in the Loyalists. But there was a chance he knew more about Walsh's disappearance, and if he did she wanted to find out what it was.

Luke put down his rod and helped the boys reel their lines in.

"Are we quitting?" Jayden couldn't hide the disappointment in her voice.

Luke smiled. He'd heard it, too. "No, we're ready for lunch."

Had she been sitting here for—she glanced at her watch—nearly four hours? She got to her feet as Luke gave the boys hand wipes from a plastic container. Popping the lid on the cooler, Jayden began passing out sandwiches. The boys took their food and juice to the front of the boat where they could hang over the side and pretend to see their next catch. Luke dropped into the seat next to her.

"Are you bored?"

"You've got to be kidding. I get to sit and relax while you entertain the boys. No dishes to wash, no animals to mend, no floors to clean. If this is bored, I'll take more."

"Good."

He bit into his sandwich, and they both chewed in silence. They didn't speak again until they'd finished their food. Then Luke leaned back in the seat, stretching his legs out in front him. She couldn't help but notice the carved muscles beneath his light brown hair.

"I'm glad it's not hot."

Jayden nodded. "Feels like fall."

"It is fall."

"I know, but that doesn't mean it's not going to feel like July."

They were both quiet again.

"What made your sister adopt the two boys? Or is that too private for me to ask?" Luke finally asked.

"No, it's okay. She and her husband hadn't been able to have kids. Caitland knew the boys' mother. She and my sister had been friends in school. She got mixed up with drugs. My sister didn't see her for a few years—the boys were only babies when Caitland ran into her again. Garrett was only a few months old." Jayden leaned closer to him and lowered her voice. "She offered to sell them to Caitland. Caitland knew the boys would be better off with her, so she and Robert officially adopted them. The girl took the money and signed them over."

"Does she ever try to see them?"

"No. They never heard from the boys' mother again. They tried to find her, but any family she'd once had here had either died or disappeared."

"Do the boys know?"

"About the money or about being adopted?"

Luke raised an eyebrow and Jayden gave him a half smile. "Okay, that was a stupid question."

"Yeah, since it would be kind of obvious to them, at least by this age, that they weren't exactly your sister and brother-in-law's children."

"Right. But they don't know about the money, and we don't plan to tell them. We say their mother was sick and couldn't take care of them anymore, which is the truth."

"And now they've lost another set of parents."

She stared at Luke's legs, only inches away from her own, and propped her elbow on her thigh so she could rest her head in her hand. It felt too heavy to hold up right now.

Luke put his hand on her other leg but Jayden didn't flinch when he touched her this time. Rather, she felt a liquid heat spread from his hand to the rest of her body.

"I'm sorry to bring up that subject."

"We've all got to deal with it."

"I didn't intend for you to have to deal with it today, with me."

She glanced to the front of the boat where the boys had started fishing on their own.

"The more we talk about it now, the sooner we'll get past how hard it is. We try to remember the good times. Or at least that's what the therapist tells us to do."

"I didn't know the boys were in therapy."

"Oh, yeah. As soon as I got here we all started. It's helped a lot. My sister should have had the boys in it before now."

"Why? Do they have problems being adopted?"

"Maybe a little, I guess any kid would. But they have problems with other kids being mean to them, your wonderful Militia clients' kids."

She felt rather than saw Luke's reaction and she wished she could take the words back. She hadn't wanted to spoil the moment, but it was too late. He started to pull his hand away from her leg. But she stopped him, covering his hand with hers. She looked up, and he was staring at her. Mesmerized by his dark gaze, it was as if she was falling into the ocean. He turned his hand to grasp her fingers, rubbing his thumb across the back of her hand.

A rush of desire hit her and she was shocked at the force of it. The sounds around them dipped to a low hum and all she could hear was her own heart hammering and Luke's ragged breaths. This was ridiculous. They were holding hands, yet parts of her body ached as though he'd actually been touching them. He leaned in, closing the distance between them and effectively stopping her breath in her throat. Was he going to kiss her?

"Hey, Mr. Luke, I got another fish!"

Luke straightened, and Jayden breathed. He let go of her hand and briefly cupped the side of her neck as he stood. Then he was gone to help the boys. Falling against the back of the seat she took a huge gulp of her hot soda. What was she doing here? He was the enemy right? At the moment a part of her was beginning to believe she could be wrong about him.

JAYDEN DROVE LUKE'S TRUCK forward while he and the boys stood beside the boat launch. After nearly five hours on the water, they'd had enough fishing. When she stopped, the boys climbed in the backseat and she jumped out to let Luke behind the wheel.

She heard the roar of the engine before the sheriff's car rolled into sight. It skidded to a stop in front of them and she glanced back at Luke, who'd been securing the boat.

Pete climbed from the vehicle with the engine still running.

"Man, I've been hunting you for hours," he said to Luke.

"I brought the boys fishing and left my cell phone at home so I could get a little peace."

"I hate to interrupt, but you'll need to get to the sheriff's office as soon as you can."

"What's up?"

"Duke Swayze's dead."

## CHAPTER EIGHT

LUKE HAD FLUNG OPEN his door before the truck completely stopped rolling. Jayden jumped to the ground, not wanting to give him reason to pause and consider the fact that he'd let her come with him. After Pete's explosive news, they'd gone straight to Luke's house to drop off the boat, and he didn't hesitate when she said she wanted to drop the boys off at her mother's so she could go with him. She'd expected him to put up a fight.

When they reached the sheriff's office, Luke held the door open for her. As they went through, his hand pressed against the small of her back. The hallway opened to a large room with several desks. The low hum of activity inside was punctuated by the occasional loud voice. Jayden ignored the questioning glances, heading straight for Matt Wright's office at the opposite end of the room.

The somewhat menacing figure of Jackson Cooper filled one of the wooden chairs and he lifted an eyebrow when she entered. The other quickly followed when Luke came in right behind her, his fingertips still grazing her back. She was here for information and wasn't concerned with the investigator's opinion so long as it didn't get her kicked out.

"What's she doing here?"

Jayden turned to Sheriff Wright. She hadn't expected him to protest.

"She was with me when I got the news and she wanted to come," Luke explained. "Is there a problem?"

"I don't usually have an audience when I meet with the public defender. I doubt you want the details all over the community."

"I wouldn't spread gossip." Jayden knotted her hands into fists. She'd always liked Matt. Why was he giving her a hard time now?

"She's working as my assistant on this case. She won't repeat anything she hears."

The two officers gave Luke a questioning look and, to be honest, Jayden had to struggle to keep from spinning around to stare at him.

"The vet is your legal assistant?" One corner of Jackson Cooper's mouth turned upward.

She could feel Luke stiffen behind her.

"That's right. You have something to say about it?"

Cooper waved his hands in the air. "Not me. Whatever you want is fine."

Matt nodded. "All right then. This afternoon when they made rounds, the guards found Duke Swayze had hanged himself in his cell with the bedsheet."

"Suicide?"

Jayden turned slightly to see Luke as he spoke.

Matt shrugged. "That's what it looked like. He was alone in the cell and had been since we picked him up. The door was locked. What do you think? Ever see anything to make you believe Swayze was suicidal?"

"I don't know. He seemed mentally unstable on occasion, but I saw no indication he was suicidal. It is possible, though."

"Unstable on occasion?" The words slipped out before Jayden could stop them. She saw the confused look on Jackson Cooper's face and wondered if it mirrored her own. Swayze was trouble, but she figured he liked himself way too much to commit suicide. She had to bite her lip to keep from saying so.

Luke ignored her outburst and continued. "Did he have problems with any of the other inmates that you two might know about? He never mentioned it to me, but maybe you heard of it."

Matt and Jackson both shook their heads.

"What about the guard in the jail? Had he given any of them a hard time?"

Matt stiffened. "Now, wait a minute. My people didn't have anything to do with this."

"He obviously wasn't monitored closely enough."

"He was monitored the same as everyone else."

"So how did he hang himself?"

Matt raked a hand through his hair, and Jayden could see his frustration building. "We don't have a lot of people being held down there. No one was in the cells near his. We had no idea he was a danger to himself or he'd have been on a suicide watch. If you thought he might do this you should have told us."

"I assume you're sending the body for an autopsy."

"Of course we are. State crime lab will be here to pick him up this evening."

"Good. Let me know as soon as you get a report." Luke pulled her from the room as he left. She wanted to protest. She hadn't heard enough yet, but until the autopsy was complete there'd likely be nothing else but speculation. She followed him, keeping quiet until she slammed the truck door behind her.

"Your assistant?"

Luke shrugged as he started the engine. "You wanted to be in there and I had to give them a decent reason."

"You don't think Duke Swayze killed himself, do you? I know he was paranoid at times, but surely he wouldn't hurt himself."

"I don't know. He became depressed in jail."

"That's absurd. You know perfectly well the Militia had him killed. Maybe he knew too much. Who knows? But they got to him as sure as anything."

"You heard the sheriff. There's no sign of foul play. Swayze was Militia, but that doesn't mean he was carrying out a job for them. I don't have any reason to think they were involved in this."

She twisted in the seat to stare at him. "Why are you protecting them?"

"I'm not protecting anyone, but I'm not jumping to wild conclusions, either."

As he pulled onto the highway toward her house, she kept quiet and watched two girls riding bikes along the sidewalk. Arguing with Luke about this was a lost cause. If he was being paid by the Militia he'd never admit they were responsible for Duke's death.

She bumped against the door as Luke wheeled into her mother's drive faster than he should have. She pulled at the handle when the truck jerked to a stop.

"Thanks for taking the boys fishing."

"Thanks for letting them go. I enjoyed it."

She watched him for a moment but he stared straight ahead, so she slid out and slammed the door shut. He gunned the truck and sped back the way he'd come. She was surprised to find her feet dragging as she climbed the steps to her mother's front door. They'd had a nice day and for a short time she'd even forgotten about Luke's affiliation with the Loyalists. But, she reminded herself, that was something she didn't need to forget.

THE SKY WAS OVERCAST and he raced along the trail, occasionally stumbling, even though he knew the path well. Luke sprinted up the two uneven steps and barely caught himself before he rushed into the cabin. He couldn't afford to look as if he was panicked. His knock was followed by a muffled voice and he pushed open the door then pulled it closed behind him.

"So, Taylor, what's the problem?"

"Duke Swayze's dead."

Joseph Bergeron leaned back in his chair. "I heard. Sounds more like a problem solved."

Fighting the urge to pace the room, Luke took a seat across the table from the other man. "Was Swayze that dangerous to the Loyalists?"

"He had potential to be. He knew more than he should and he wasn't reliable up here." Bergeron tapped his head. "He committed suicide. It's one less headache."

Luke smacked his hand on the table, and the sound vibrated in the air. "Duke Swayze might have been mentally unstable in a lot of ways, but I don't think he would commit suicide."

The other man pressed his weight against the back of the chair, his black eyes sparking in the dim light. "You need to remember that I tell you what to think, and I don't ever want to hear you say that again. From now on, as far as you're concerned, Swayze killed himself and you won't be surprised. You might even have had suspicions that he'd do it."

"If I'd had those thoughts I should have reported them. I'll get in trouble."

"Maybe you weren't sure it was important since he was always saying crazy stuff anyway."

Luke wanted to shout. He didn't need this guy telling him what to think. But Bergeron was in charge, and as far as the Loyalist leader was concerned, he had every right to tell Luke how he needed to handle this situation. He was sure the other man felt he paid the lawyer very well to do his bidding, and he was right. So Luke only nodded and watched Bergeron smile, satisfied.

"Now, for something important."

Luke had a hard time paying attention to Bergeron. In a matter of minutes, Duke Swayze's existence had been relegated to less importance than the next item of business. Then Bergeron's words pierced his thoughts.

"How much do you think the Miller girl knows about what that reporter was doing?"

"Miller girl? Are you talking about Jayden Miller?"

"Haven't you been listening to me? Of course I'm talking about her. You two have been seen around together, which isn't a bad move, I might add. What does she know?"

Luke shook his head, more to clear it than to indicate Jayden's knowledge. "If she knows anything, she hasn't told me. But then we're not exactly sharing secrets. Her nephew is on my baseball team."

"So taking her fishing wasn't a way to get information from her."

"Uh, no. I did it for the two boys. It looks good for me to do that kind of thing in the community." Luke wanted to kick himself for thinking, even for an instant, that the bosses had relaxed their vigilance over him. He'd thought they trusted him, but wasn't sure how long they'd buy the "I need to look good in the community" story. Being seen with a woman who was raising children of mixed race would bring trouble on him, a lot of trouble.

Bergeron slid his plastic cup back and forth on the table. "I'm thinking if you stuck with it, the two of you might start—what did you say?—sharing secrets. For us, that would be very helpful."

"Let me get this straight. You want me to get close to her to see what she knows about Eric Walsh's work?"

"That's right. Can you deal with her and those two brats for a little longer?"

Luke appeared unmoved on the outside, while his insides churned with anger. "I can do it. I think it's a waste of time, though. If she had information, she'd tell the police. She's that kind of person."

"You think, just like that—" Bergeron snapped his fingers "—you've got a handle on what kind of person she is?"

Luke couldn't help shifting uncomfortably in his chair.

"Well, yeah, I believe I can tell."

Bergeron laughed. "You might be surprised by her, but we'll see. Find out what she knows and I'll send you a bonus to help make you feel better about wasting your time."

Luke nodded and stood to leave. Bergeron figured sending him extra money would make using Jayden easier, which of course it wouldn't. But if he did this and could tell them she didn't know anything, then maybe they'd leave her and the boys alone. He could help them stay safe and still do his job. He didn't tell Bergeron how much he was going to enjoy this assignment, probably because he didn't want to admit it to himself.

JAYDEN SAT BEHIND the receptionist's desk in the front room of the clinic. Her partner was eating lunch with his wife in his office and the receptionist had left to run errands. Jayden tapped at the computer, concentrating on updating records. She looked up when the front door opened and her fingers froze. Amy walked in carrying a tiny puppy.

She stopped at the counter, scowling. "Are you the only one here who can wait on me?"

"Everyone's at lunch, but if you don't want me I'll go get doc from the back. He and his wife are eating."

Amy stood quietly for a minute then shrugged. "You can do it, I guess. I'm on my way to town and he's due his shots. I'd like to leave him and pick him up on my way home. Can you get that done in a couple of hours?"

"Sure, it won't be a problem."

Amy kept holding the puppy, and Jayden didn't know whether she should reach for it or not. "I'll take good care of him, I promise."

Amy nodded and handed the animal over but stayed where she was. The young, carefree girl Jayden used to know was gone and she wondered if Amy was this angry all the time, if she was happy living under the thumb of the Acadian Loyalists.

"I'd like to tell you what really happened between me and your brother."

Amy took a half step toward the door. "I know what happened."

"Then consider it my side of the story. I loved him."

Amy snorted. "Yeah, right. If you'd loved him, he'd still be here right now."

Jayden sighed, snuggling the puppy. Amy had

been about ten back then. The girl only knew what she'd been told by her father and his friends. Jayden couldn't imagine what Mr. Dubois had fabricated.

"Amy, I did love your brother. He wasn't honest with me. He wasn't honest with a lot of people. You weren't old enough to know what was happening, but I didn't make your brother do anything. I didn't even know he was in the Militia when we were in high school."

"You were both in it."

Jayden frowned. She couldn't win this argument. "I'll have your puppy ready to go when you get back."

Through the front window she watched Amy get behind the wheel of the white truck and drive away.

"You can't change years of brainwashing."

Jayden turned to see Linda Comeaux, the clinic receptionist, waiting in the doorway of the office, shaking her head. She stepped past Jayden and dropped into the chair behind the computer. "You're doing my job again, I see."

"I wasn't busy."

"Well, thanks. And don't worry about that girl. She's one mixed-up kid, not that she had a chance to be otherwise."

"I wish she'd listen to me."

"Why? It's not going to change anything."

"Maybe she'd see how dangerous her father's beliefs are and try to get away from him."

Linda swung the chair around to face Jayden. "She's not going anywhere. My late husband was a stepbrother to Paul Dubois and I used to have Amy over to our house when she was younger, but her father stopped that by the time she was twelve. I still kept up with her through friends who worked at the school. She was a smart girl and could easily have gone to college, but she'll marry Joseph Bergeron and spend the rest of her life getting smacked around every time she doesn't do exactly as he wants."

Jayden leaned against the wall. "Bergeron. I knew I recognized that man. The other day at the drugstore he was mean to the boys."

"I hate that," Linda said. "I hope one day the police, FBI or whoever, catch him and Dubois. I thought that reporter, Walsh, might get something on them but I guess that's not going to happen now."

"What's Amy doing with Bergeron?"

"She's supposed to marry him."

"He's got to be twenty-five or thirty years older than her!"

Linda nodded. "At least that. But it doesn't matter. They're living together already."

"And her father allows it?"

"I think he sort of gave her to Bergeron. She wanted to go to college, but her father wouldn't have it. He promised her to Bergeron and, when she was eighteen, that's where she went."

"Linda, that's insane. Why would she agree to that?"

"I don't imagine she had much choice."

"Couldn't she run away?"

Linda frowned. "As if they couldn't find her if they wanted to. You think you were left alone in California all these years because they didn't know where you were? I promise it was a conscious decision on their part to let you go your own way. I've been close enough to the families during the years my husband was alive to see them go after people who caused problems."

Jayden felt the cold fingers of fear on the back of her neck. She'd never been afraid of what the Militia might do to her before now. Out of sight, out of mind, she'd always thought. But now she wasn't out of sight, she was right in their face.

"I think they're involved in much more than anyone could imagine," Linda added.

"Right at the end, before Mark died," Jayden said quietly, "I was beginning to see how deep that network ran and how widespread they were. The money amazed me. They had tons of it. You wouldn't know it because they live simply, but I was with Mark when he delivered a few checks. I didn't know what they were for, only that the amounts were huge."

"Drugs and guns are big business."

"I should have known Mark was involved, that his father wouldn't have had it any other way."

"You couldn't have known what would happen."

Jayden stroked the wiggling, silky pup. "I guess not."

Linda turned her chair back to the computer. "You need to get going with that puppy or it won't be ready when Amy comes back."

Jayden nodded and went down the hall to one of

the treatment rooms. Linda might be right. Maybe she couldn't change Amy's way of thinking, but she'd like to try. She wished she could show Amy there was more for her than a man like Bergeron.

# CHAPTER NINE

LUKE FOLDED THE piece of paper and tapped it on the desk then opened it and reread it one more time. The envelope containing the letter and a wad of cash had been hand delivered by one of the Militia's usual couriers. They had two who came by periodically with money or a note telling him of their latest need. He fought the urge to wad the paper and throw it against the wall. Instead, he wheeled the rolling desk chair around and flipped on the shredder. Two hours away there was a military base in the larger town of Boyden. They wanted him to go there and talk to one of their Militia members accused of stealing from that base. What an idiot this guy was. Luke was surprised Bergeron didn't have him hanged in his cell. Just this once…. He'd had this man as a client before and he wasn't happy about dealing with him again, even if it was only "to talk."

Boyden did have a great yearly Cajun festival and he'd always wanted to go. He could get two of the Militia's jobs done at the same time. He could invite Jayden and the boys to go with him to the festival. He rolled back to his desk and picked up the phone. With his finger hovering over the button, he paused. What was he doing? This would pull Jayden and the boys deeper into the Eric Walsh disaster. However, if he could tell Bergeron they knew nothing then wouldn't they be better off? He quickly dialed.

Hearing Jayden's voice, he wanted to hang up. He was using a woman and her children to further his own cause. It was hard to believe he'd sunk so low.

"Hi, Jayden. It's Luke. I was wondering if you and the boys would like to go with me to Boyden for the festival next Saturday. I've got a meeting there, but I could drop you off and take care of my business then meet back up with you afterward. I hear it's good and they have rides for the kids."

He waited. He almost wished she'd refuse, but he couldn't afford not to get close to her. To not find out what she knew, for his sake as well as hers.

Jayden's fingers tightened around the receiver. What should she do? The boys would love to attend the festival and going with Luke would make them even happier.

"Um, let me check our calendar and make sure we don't have to be anywhere." She studied the dry-erase calendar on the wall. She scratched her finger on the empty box dated the Saturday Luke wanted them to go with him. They didn't have a thing to do.

"It looks like we're free."

He said he'd be back in touch and ended the call. If she knew for a fact that Luke was being used by the Loyalists she wouldn't consider going anywhere with him. Other than finding money in his office drawer, she didn't have any hard evidence he was involved. If she hung around him more, maybe she could get the truth. She was determined to expose Luke if he was Militia. Her subconscious nagged that she shouldn't risk the boys with him if she doubted his honesty, but she could remember how much fun the four of them had together fishing and who knew, maybe she was mistaken. Maybe getting to know Luke better wouldn't be a problem.

JAYDEN HANDED THE fluffy kitten back to the little girl.

"Now, he's had his shots and that wasn't so bad, was it?"

The girl shook her head and followed her mother from the room. Jayden heard Linda calling her from the reception area.

"I'm on my way, hold on a minute," she shouted.

Making a final sweep at the disinfectant she'd sprayed on the exam table, she tossed the used paper towel in the trash and went to the front.

"Here she is," Linda said, waving her into the waiting room where the sheriff stood waiting.

She glanced at Linda who gave a tiny shrug.

"Sheriff Wright, what's wrong?"

"I just thought you'd want to know the latest in the Walsh case."

"Yeah, I would. I've got a small office in the back—do we need to go there?"

"No. I don't guess privacy is an issue. I'm sure the

majority of the parish will know by tomorrow morning."

Jayden shifted her feet. She heard Kasey whine and glanced back at the hall door.

"None of the remains we found in the woods that day are Walsh's."

Jayden leaned against the counter for support. "But what about the watch?" Her voice came out squeaky and she wasn't sure Matt understood her because he shook his head.

"Yeah, that's the weird thing. Are you sure that was his watch?"

She nodded. "Completely sure."

"Well, we can't explain it, but we know he wasn't buried there. They've done DNA testing and nothing matches."

"That means Eric could be alive."

Matt fiddled with a pamphlet on the counter before answering. "I guess that's possible, but he could be buried elsewhere. I wanted to see if you'd meet me after work at Swayze's place and bring Kasey. Maybe we missed something there."

"Of course I'll bring him." She banged her fist against the countertop. "If Swayze were still alive we could get information from him."

"Maybe, but then again he kept his mouth shut before he committed suicide."

"Oh, please, you don't believe that for a minute, do you?"

"What else am I supposed to think? We didn't let the man get killed."

"I'm not trying to fault the sheriff's office. But if the Loyalists wanted him dead there wasn't a thing you could do. When they have an agenda nothing will stop them." Jayden paused. Her voice had gotten loud.

"Either way, we're back to square one with Walsh."

Jayden nodded. "I'll do whatever I can."

She'd start by finding out what Luke was hiding.

AFTER THREE PASSES over the yard of Duke Swayze's run-down frame house, Jayden shook her head at Matt, who shrugged.

"We'd already checked it once and didn't find anything. Just wishful thinking on my part."

Jayden turned in a circle, eyeing the trees that bordered the overgrown yard. She squinted, trying to see through the limbs. "Is that an old barn through those woods?"

"I think it is."

"I assume you checked there."

"I'm sure they did, but it wouldn't hurt to try again."

The two of them had started toward the edge of the woods when a truck spewing dust came barreling along the drive. Jayden's heart fluttered and she didn't like it. She didn't want to be glad to see Luke.

"What's he doing here?" she finally croaked.

"I called and let him know what we found. Told him we'd be giving the place a once-over if he wanted to come by."

She stared at Matt. "What would he want to do that for? It's not like he's got a client to defend. I mean, even if we find Eric's body." She didn't like the way those words sounded when they passed her lips. "Swayze's not going to trial, not on this earth anyway."

"He might have been going to defend Swayze, but he wants to find Eric, same as the rest of us."

Kasey started to wag his tail as Luke got out of the truck. Traitor dog. Luke patted the shepherd on the head as he greeted her and Matt. She shivered when his eyes darkened and hung on to her.

"We're going to check the barn through those trees," Matt explained. Luke nodded and followed along behind while Kasey trotted at her side.

As the dog moved through the trees and brush, Luke stayed right next to her, making Jayden fidget with her hair then Kasey's leash. Matt had stepped several feet away to take a call on his cell phone.

"I'm glad you agreed to go to the festival with me next week."

"Thanks for asking us. The boys will enjoy it."

"I hope you'll enjoy it, too."

Luke's voice had dropped an octave, even steamier than his usual sexy tone. It made her uncomfortable yet excited, and she didn't need that from Luke.

"I'm sure I'll like it. I haven't been since I was a kid."

She hurried toward Kasey, who was steadily sniffing the ground. Thankfully, Matt had finished his call and walked over to Luke before the lawyer could follow her.

Her relief was short-lived when Matt gave a slight wave and shouted, "I've got to get back to the office." Then he disappeared through the trees toward his cruiser. Luke stayed where he was and let her work the dog. She rounded the barn and when she came back to the front he was gone. She tried to peer through the brush to see if he was at the house but it was too thick. Then she heard boards clattering inside the old barn.

"Jayden, come here."

She hurried toward the opening of the building and hoped the roof wouldn't collapse on them. Luke was at the back, his feet hanging in the air as he sat at the edge of the old hay loft.

"Climb up and look at this."

She glanced from him to the ancient ladder he'd propped against the decayed rafter.

"That ladder is a piece of junk."

"It held me."

"And that was a miracle."

"It's stronger than it looks. Now come on."

She put her foot on the bottom rung and tested it with her weight. It didn't creak or groan so she climbed until she could see where Luke was sitting. A dusty pile of hay had been pushed next to the wall covering the bottom half of large cracks in the rotting boards.

She fingered a piece of the dried straw. "There shouldn't be hay in here. It's obvious no one's used this barn for a long time but this isn't that old."

"Kind of like it was put here, huh?"

She narrowed her eyes. "Why would anyone do that?"

He leaned to the side and pointed to the cracks. From this height they had a clear view of Duke Swayze's house. Luke poked into the pile of straw with a stick and spread it around. Mixed in with the straw were candy wrappers and an empty soda bottle.

Jayden looked at the wall. "Someone's been watching the house. Do you think it could have been Eric?"

"I can't think who else would want to sit here, can you?"

"No, I can't. Not unless the Militia had it in for Swayze before he was ever arrested."

Luke didn't answer and the skin on Jayden's neck tingled. "You think that might be it?"

He jerked his head around and looked at her.

"What? Oh, no. I doubt it was the Militia, more likely Walsh trying to snoop. Maybe Duke caught him here. We better get down. I'll call the sheriff. We're contaminating evidence as it is."

As soon as they reached the ground, Luke got on the phone and she headed for her truck. He'd looked surprised when she'd mentioned the Militia, but since Swayze was dead maybe there was more going on than one man's insanity. Jayden still couldn't believe the suicide story.

Luke caught up to her in the rutted drive as she was opening the door on the passenger side of the old truck for Kasey.

"I've got to hang around until Officer Cooper can get here to start collecting evidence."

"I'm surprised they didn't find it the first time they searched."

"I think they were concentrating under the ground rather than above it."

"That's true, I guess." She patted the seat and Kasey jumped in and immediately stretched out.

Luke's fingers closed on her upper arm. "Stay and keep me company until Cooper gets here."

"I need to get home."

"The boys aren't there. Your mom took them to an early movie as soon as they got out of school."

"How do you know that? No one told me."

"I called her looking for you when I heard about Walsh. I was supposed to give you the message. I completely forgot."

Jayden frowned. She didn't like Luke knowing more about her family than she did. It was like he was worming his way into the hearts of her mother and the boys. Worming his way into their hearts? Now she was being melodramatic.

"Is the decision that difficult?"

"I shouldn't. I have lots of laundry to do."

"You're turning me down for laundry? That's cruel."

She couldn't keep from laughing. "Oh, all right, I'll wait with you until Jackson gets here." She pushed past him and went to the back of her truck. Letting the tailgate down, she lifted herself onto it. Instead of sitting, Luke leaned his hip against the edge. She wished he'd sit because this way he loomed over her, making her feel small and vulnerable.

"Every time I think we're getting along you suddenly act as if you wouldn't spit on me if I were on fire."

She snorted at the image. He shifted his feet and

his thigh pressed against her knee, easily killing her amusement.

"What difference does it make whether or not I like you?"

"I'd think, since you've agreed to spend an entire day with me, you must at least find me tolerable."

"That's for the boys. They like you and they need a man in their lives. You're Elliot's baseball coach, too, and that makes you doubly special to him. Though none of us are happy about how things turned out with Caitland and Robert's case."

Luke sighed and rubbed his eyes. When his hand fell away she saw oceans of what could have been sadness. "I did what I had to do."

She gripped the edge of the tailgate next to her legs. "And you did it so well."

"I have a responsibility to my clients."

She rubbed a finger across a bolt. She was tired of this battle. Everyone else had let go of what had happened after her sister and brother-in-law's accident. She was also growing tired of finding reasons not to like all the things she saw in Luke that were, well, so likeable.

Before she realized it, he'd moved and, with his fingers, he pushed her ponytail back over her shoulder.

"I'm sorry it turned out the way it did with the case. I didn't want to see the guy go free. I knew Caitland and Robert and I wanted justice served. But I had nothing to do with the lost evidence."

His hand had finally came to rest on her thigh.

They both seemed to notice it at the same time and his fingers pressed against her khaki pants and burned straight through to her skin. With his other hand, he caught a strand of hair that had blown against her cheek and tucked it behind her ear then traced her neck. Oh, no, he was going to kiss her. She should have jumped and run as fast as she could. Instead, she leaned forward. Her lips met his briefly, a slight touch before his hand tightened on her neck and tugged her closer to him. She imagined she felt the rough, strong fingers tremble against her skin as she met his tongue with her own, hungrily deepening the kiss.

Still standing, he moved to straddle her leg and the strength and heat of his desire warmed her thigh. She whimpered as he slowly teased her lips and tongue with his own until her body cried out for more, for him to touch her everywhere. His breathing became erratic and she had to concentrate to remember to get a breath herself.

He pulled back and looked at her, his chest rising and falling. She could barely think coherently, but she knew she'd never been this out of control with any man before. And she wasn't so sure she liked it. In truth she did like it, but it also scared her to death. It was time to make a getaway while she still could. If he kissed her any more the deputies might find them sprawled in the bed of her truck. Pushing him aside and springing to the ground, she hurried to the driver's side door.

"I've got to go." Her voice cracked and she

wanted to kick herself for sounding like a schoolgirl after her first kiss.

He nodded and slammed her tailgate shut then moved to shut the passenger door. In her haste, she might have driven off with the door open. She glanced once at Luke expecting to see him smiling or at least gloating. Instead his eyes barely met hers and for a moment she thought she might have even seen a flash of fear. But she was surely imagining things, because men like Luke didn't show fear. As she sped down the drive she could see him in the rearview mirror leaning against his own truck.

He couldn't watch her leave or he might jump in his vehicle and take off after her. He didn't know whether to apologize for the kiss or ask for more. Kissing her wasn't required for him to find out if she knew more about the reporter than she was telling. Putting his lips on hers had simply been his desire run amok. And he had to be in control. Passion was a luxury he couldn't afford.

He'd done a lot of wrong things for the sake of his job. He always justified it that way: for his job. But he was getting tired of trying to excuse himself when he knew he was wrong. He wasn't so sure anymore that this was where he'd intended his life to go. That case involving the man whose drunk driving had killed Jayden's sister and brother-in-law had been like that. It was a horrible and ugly thing, but he'd been a party to it for the sake of his job. If she ever found out, she'd hate him because there'd be no excuse good enough. He didn't want to imagine what the boys would think when they were old enough to understand. He wasn't the one who'd made the evidence disappear, but he knew who was responsible. Without evidence there was no case, and that was exactly what the Militia had wanted.

Tires crunching on the gravel drive caught his attention and he saw the sheriff's cruisers approaching. He kicked a rock across the ground. He didn't like Luke Taylor very much today.

## CHAPTER TEN

LUKE EASED INTO the wooden chair across the table from the young man. The situation wasn't right. The Loyalists had clearly been unfolding a plan, and he hadn't seen it happening. He had thought the Militia trusted him. He recognized today that he was only allowed to know what they wanted him to and nothing more. He felt as if he'd done nothing in two years except compromise every value he had.

"Hey, Taylor, looks like you got me again."

William Lebeaux was nearly twenty-six, but he looked and often acted about fifteen. Yet he'd been arrested for a very grown-up crime.

"How hard you think it'll be to get me off'n this one?"

In his mind his fist flew across the table and knocked the boy out of the chair on his butt. He tried to keep his cool.

"Will, I'm not your lawyer this time. Bergeron only sent me here to talk to you. I don't imagine the government's going to make it very easy for you to get off. Breaking and entering on a military base wasn't the smartest thing you'll ever do."

"You got me off last time. Course, I know the Militia helped when they made off with all that evidence. It was a mistake. Those people weren't supposed to get hurt. They got in the way."

"They got in the way of you driving drunk, you mean."

Will shrugged and studied the back of his hand. Luke didn't want to hear this, especially since he was falling in love with Jayden. He had to admit that it could be happening and he didn't want to stop it, not yet. His work couldn't stop now, either, not when he was this close.

"It was my job to defend you during that case."

"So what does Bergeron want?" The boy tapped the table then looked up with a smile that revealed his stained, chipped teeth. "He needs what I know, huh? I told him on the phone, when I get outta here I'll give him the information, then he can give me enough money to skip town."

"You can't leave town. This is a federal charge. They'll be looking for you."

"So I'll leave the country. Don't matter to me none. I'll go down to Mexico."

Luke scratched notes on a piece of paper. "Why don't you tell me everything that happened. I might be able to help your lawyer. The police say you broke into the computer room and were downloading documents."

The young man nodded. "They were pretty confused about that one. Guess I don't look much like a computer nerd, huh? They couldn't understand why I wasn't over trying to get the weapons. If I'd been there for myself, maybe I would have gone for the guns, but you and I know I had bigger fish to fry than any gun."

"Yeah, but did you get it?" Luke's hand paused over the paper automatically, then he forced it to keep moving. He didn't look up for fear the boy might see that he didn't know what he'd been after. But he was about to.

"I said I did, didn't I? All the security information about the visit, the schedules—everything." Without warning his hand shot across the table and caught Luke's wrist, effectively stopping his writing.

"I see what's goin' on here. Bergeron sent you to get the information from me so he can leave me in this jail and not pay me. But you tell him I'm not saying a word 'til I get loose. If they leave me here and try to do the job without me, I'll be screaming my story to every cop I see. You tell them that."

Luke slammed his notebook closed and dropped it in his briefcase. "I'll tell them."

He wanted to go to the festival and spend the day with Jayden and the boys without having to think about plots and schedules or who might die next, if it might be him or someone close to him.

This was the reason he'd never wanted a relationship with anyone since Alicia. Now, at the worst possible time, he was drawing closer to Jayden. Danger would trail her family simply because they were near him. But if he didn't keep them close, they could get hurt anyway and he might not see it coming.

At his truck he flung his case under the backseat. He'd never felt pulled in so many different directions. When he'd been engaged to Alicia, they'd at least had the same goal, the same purpose. She'd lost her life chasing that goal and he tried not to give much thought to the fact that he could be killed in the same pursuit. Up to this point it hadn't been relevant. Today, for the first time in a long time, it mattered.

JAYDEN WEAVED HER WAY through the crowd until she could see Luke sitting on a bench waiting for them. They'd arranged to meet at the park in the center of the area where the festival was being held. She hurried on with Garrett and Elliot beside her. He looked hot even in the shade of the huge oak.

"You must have finished early. Have you been here long?"

"A few minutes."

He stood and the boys immediately hit him with their list of rides.

"Why haven't you done any of them already?"

They looked at her pointedly, but didn't say a word.

"It's me, okay? I don't like fair rides, maybe the Ferris wheel but not much else."

"You're a chicken. I would never have thought you'd be a chicken."

Elliot giggled and Garrett put a hand over his mouth.

She took a step closer to Luke who was flanked by the two boys. Darn, these men were ganging up on her already.

"I am not a chicken. I just don't do rides. Now let's go."

She turned and marched toward the midway where the music blasted and mechanical equipment whirred. Behind her she heard the muffled word "chicken" again. She spun around and glared at Luke who was smiling innocently while the boys doubled over laughing. She'd show him who was chicken.

Thirty minutes later, sandwiched between her nephews and Luke, she screamed between breaths of laughter as a machine dubbed the Super Himalaya spun them so fast they all slid to one side of the seat and were crushed against Luke. His arm linked behind her, his hand on the back of Garrett's neck. Fighting the centrifugal force, he bent his head near her ear. "I kind of like this. Can we do it again?"

She turned to answer, but his lips caught hers briefly before he was pulled away as the ride operator kicked up the speed another notch.

The four of them stumbled through the throng of people after it was over.

"Let's get ice cream," Elliot suggested.

She groaned. "You couldn't possibly want to eat. Not after that." She waved her hand behind them at the ride, which was beginning to whirl its new load.

But the boys bounded ahead.

"They must have spotted the ice cream on the way over here."

She didn't answer Luke, but tried to keep an eye on the kids. She didn't want to lose sight of them here. She was scared she'd never find them again.

Then another good reason to keep them close appeared. Joseph Bergeron was approaching them from the opposite direction with Amy walking behind him.

"Oh, no." She didn't notice she'd said the words aloud until Luke stiffened beside her. The moment might pass without incident. The man and woman might walk past…but of course that didn't happen. Bergeron sidestepped in front of Elliot and Garrett, cutting them off. Jayden tried to run but her legs were frozen. It didn't matter because Luke was there before she could get her mind and body to work in unison. She could see the anger that whipped across Bergeron's face. Luke didn't budge, his upper body stiff and pulling against the fabric of his T-shirt as he put himself between Bergeron and the boys. When she reached them, whatever it had been was over. Bergeron moved on, but when he passed her, he whispered something under his breath she was certain wasn't "good afternoon."

The boys clung to Luke. Garrett openly gripped a fistful of his shirt while Elliot attempted to give off the air of someone older and unperturbed. But she could see his shoulder buried into Luke's waist even while they walked away.

At the ice cream stand, the boys waited to order while she and Luke looked on.

"Thanks for standing up for them."

Luke shifted his weight from side to side before answering. "Does that happen often?"

"That's only the second incident since I've been

here, but it was with the same person. I've heard Elliot say they get harassed at school, but usually by the same few kids. Most of the students don't give their background a second thought. In the end I'm afraid they'll have to deal with that problem forever—from certain people."

Luke nodded. "Maybe so, but they won't deal with it while I'm around."

She was still surprised that he'd go against the Militia. If he was working for them, wouldn't it jeopardize his paycheck? The man beside her didn't seem worried that he'd stood up to one of the biggest Loyalist members in the area.

"Come on. Let's forget it and try to enjoy the rest of the afternoon."

She nodded, but her mind was whirling. Maybe Luke wasn't working with the Militia. He certainly wasn't acting like it. She'd never be happier about being wrong.

LUKE WATCHED JAYDEN clean up the sleeping Garrett. Elliot, who'd awakened when they stopped at the house, had gotten into the shower. Garrett didn't budge. When she finished wiping away the worst of the day's dirt, she pulled his covers up. They checked on Elliot, who'd finished his shower and was asleep in his own room.

In the living room, Jayden fell back onto the sofa.

"Whew, that was a long day," Luke said as he dropped beside her.

She grinned. "Yes, it was. But we had fun. Thanks for asking us."

He didn't want the evening to end and was surprised by the thought. He settled deeper into the cushions.

"I'm glad you came. I wasn't so sure you'd agree."

"You have to understand that it's a big object to get past. I mean, of all the women interested in you around here, why me? Is it because you feel bad about what happened with Caitland and Robert?"

He turned to face her. "I don't always like the way things turn out, Jayden, but that's the way it goes."

She nodded. "I guess you have to take the good with the bad."

"Yes, you do. I promise that my interest in you and the boys has nothing to do with that."

She squirmed on the cushions and he put a hand on her leg. "This makes you uncomfortable, doesn't it?"

She pulled her leg beneath her. "It's hard to know if I can believe you or trust you because of your involvement with the Loyalists."

"What makes you say I'm *involved* with them? I take cases for a dozen other people not in the Loyalists, too."

"But that guy, Speck, was in your office the other day. I know he's Militia. He has been since I was a kid."

Luke didn't respond right away. He needed to scramble his brain a bit to get his answers. He hadn't expected her to know Speck or question what the guy was doing with him.

"He was checking with me about Swayze. They were related."

"I didn't know."

She opened her mouth but snapped it shut.

"Go ahead and say what's on your mind. I can tell there's more."

She hesitated. "I snooped in your desk drawer the other day and found a lot of cash. Right after Speck had left. I thought—I mean—is the Militia paying you off to help their people?"

Jayden had trespassed.... Luke had never found holding his composure this difficult. As if her transgression wasn't enough, it put him in the unwanted position of having to lie to her. Again. One more story, one more lie, what was the difference at this point?

"That was payment for a four-wheeler I sold. I'd had several for a while, but I decided to get rid of one. A guy paid me in cash that morning and I hadn't had time to take it to the bank."

Jayden rubbed her hand across her forehead and her look of embarrassment made his fabrication even worse.

"I'm sorry. I shouldn't have been going through your things and I shouldn't have jumped to conclusions."

He got to his feet and looked down at her. "You're right, you shouldn't have."

"I'm sorry," she repeated. "I knew you'd be mad but I had to ask."

"I can understand your mistrust but I'm not what you think."

He turned and left, resisting the urge to slam the door behind him. He hated being in the middle of this mess and he resented Jayden for putting him in the position of straight out lying to her. He tried to remind himself that his job and everything about him was a sham, but that the deception was for a good cause. What was honest was his feelings for Jayden, her family and the people in Cypress Landing.

He might have gotten himself in trouble with Bergeron today. The man had turned red when Luke stepped between him and the boys. He'd smooth it over, but Bergeron wouldn't be happy, especially when he found out Luke had no information from Jayden or the boys about Walsh. He hadn't even asked them yet. Sooner or later he'd have to start digging. He figured he might as well make it sooner.

LUKE TURNED THE KEY in the lock and pushed open the door leading from his garage into the kitchen. He hadn't left a light on and the house was dark but as the latch clicked behind him his muscles instinctively tightened. His hand slid down to his calf but found nothing there. Damn, he hadn't worn a gun today, with Elliot and Garrett around. Moving along the counter he opened a drawer and patted inside until he found a pistol. One of several he kept stashed around his house, in case he needed it. Like now. On the other side of the kitchen a long bar separated him from the living room. He squatted until he could just see over the edge of the counter. In the other room, a man sat in his recliner. Luke bent low and raced across the room, hitting the light switch with one hand and leveling the pistol with the other.

"You're a little slow, Taylor. If I'd wanted to take you out, my men would have done it outside and not waited for you to get in here."

Lowering his weapon, Luke faked a mask of calm arrogance. "You must have something important as hell to discuss with me to come to my house. Your being seen here won't do me or the Militia any good."

He sat on the sofa and tossed the gun on the coffee table. Bergeron had to believe he wasn't scared of him. Respectful but not scared.

"You're in hot water and I'm giving you a chance to explain yourself before you end up bait in the bottom of the river."

"I don't know what you're talking about." He did, of course, but unless he played this exactly right Bergeron wouldn't buy it.

"Like hell you don't. Pushing me around in a public place over a couple of half-breed kids will get you killed. If it had been anyone else it would have happened before they ever made it back to their car."

The man was despicable and deserved much worse than being pushed around in public. Hopefully, he'd be getting that very soon.

"How do expect me to get Jayden or those two kids to trust me enough to tell me anything if I don't take up for the boys when they're in trouble. I'm trying to do the job you assigned me. If you're going to harass those two then I've got to do what a man dating their aunt would. She's already seen Speck at my office and is suspicious of my connection with the Loyalists."

Across from him Bergeron leaned back in his chair and scratched his head. Outside the crickets chirped and two owls carried on a conversation that gave Luke an eerie feeling. Though out of sight, Bergeron's men weren't far away and he knew they were simply waiting for a sign to end his life.

The other man slapped his hand on his leg and smiled.

"You're right. You do have to play the hero for her and her rug rats. I don't like it, but we need to find out what Walsh knew and if he shared it. Who knows, we might even find him."

"So, you heard his body wasn't one recovered from the woods?"

"Probably before you did."

Luke didn't doubt that at all. "Are you sure no one with the Loyalists has an idea what happened to Walsh?"

"I imagine Swayze killed him. Walsh visited him at his house. The reporter thought he was doing good getting friendly with Duke."

"I thought you said you didn't order Swayze to take care of Walsh."

"I didn't, but Swayze said he killed him, so I guess he did. I only wish we'd known that Walsh's body wasn't out there before Swayze died. I'd like to know exactly what he did with him, just to be on the safe side."

"And you're certain he killed him."

"I guess we can't be certain about anything when we don't have a body. He reported he did the job, but never said where, only jabbered a lot of his usual crazy stuff."

Luke decided Bergeron had calmed down enough to change the subject.

"I met with your man who was caught on that military base today. He says to tell you he's not giving any information until we get him out of there and he gets his money."

"Does he now? That boy's been nothing but trouble. If he wasn't good with a computer and Dubois' nephew I'd have done away with him long ago. But he can forget it. We have what we need without him."

"He says if you don't get him out and you try to do the job without him, he'll tell the police."

"What job was he talking about?"

"He didn't tell me, only said he'd give the information to you and no one else. I assumed you'd know what he meant."

"I do. Let's make sure his lawyer gets him out on bail and I'll take care of it after that."

Bergeron continued to study him. Luke ignored the urge to look away until the other man heaved himself to his feet.

"You're doing good work, Taylor. Now get what you can from that Miller girl or those kids and you'll have earned your keep."

He left through the back French doors without

bothering to explain how he'd gotten inside in the first place. It didn't matter. They'd have knocked the door down if it had suited them. He watched through the glass as the men disappeared into the woods past his backyard. The moonlight reflected in the pool and Luke ripped off his clothes and stepped into the cool night air. He dove into the water, wishing he'd find Jayden standing there when he came up for air. Fantasies were the last thing he needed. On the other hand, he did need to know every detail about her. He'd have to be careful, though. He was getting too attached and he couldn't have that.

# CHAPTER ELEVEN

LUKE PUSHED THE four-wheeler past the front of the barn. Running an all-terrain vehicle in the middle of the night wouldn't worry a soul. Not that he expected to be heard. His house sat in the middle of fifty acres, which itself was surrounded by a large wooded property owned by a man who lived in another state. He started the engine and thumbed the throttle, setting off toward the edge of the trees.

The trail he was on narrowed and tree limbs slapped at his body until he could go no farther on the ATV. He climbed off and negotiated the rest of the path on foot. Dew wet the black long-sleeve T-shirt he wore and it lay cool against his skin. He veered left then right, the opposite way from how he'd come last time. The trees thinned and he could see the barn, but he stayed on the edge of the woods circling the area. When he reached the overgrown dirt road, he noted the car he was expecting. Luke continued several hundred yards down the road to make sure no other vehicles were hiding before he started toward the dilapidated structure.

Charles Greer was leaning against the wall when Luke slipped through the broken door.

"It's about time you showed. What took you so long?"

"I had to make sure you weren't followed."

The man snorted. "Do you think I'd have come if I thought I was being followed?"

"I'm being cautious, old man."

"Not too old to kick your butt."

Luke laughed, waving his hands defensively. "Hey, I believe you."

Charles straightened and Luke could see his smile in the slivers of moonlight that found their way through the holes in the tin roof.

"What's new in Militia land, Luke?"

"Bergeron didn't give Swayze the order to kill the reporter."

"You think Swayze acted on his own?"

"No, the order came from higher up."

"Dubois?"

Luke shook his head. "Not him, maybe another player even more important, because Bergeron didn't agree with what happened and he doesn't seem sure Walsh is dead. We don't have a body."

"That's true, but we still believe Swayze was ordered to kill the reporter. You're saying it was a person or persons more important than Bergeron or Dubois, maybe from another Militia group?"

Luke nodded. "That's exactly what I'm thinking. When I met with Bergeron he wouldn't tell me. He figured I didn't need to know."

"You think it's the same group we've been trailing for the past five years?"

"I do. They're working on a major project together, though I can't imagine what it would be in this area."

Charles rattled the keys in his pocket. "I'll get our team doing a little research."

"We need it. I don't know if I can get into that inner circle in time to find out what's happening."

The older man was silent for a minute before he said, "How are you holding up?"

Luke tilted his head, but he couldn't see Charles's features clearly. "I'm good, why?"

"You've been undercover for a while now. You've got no friends because you aren't really you, and you have no contacts through the Bureau except me."

Luke moved to the door of the barn and surveyed the distance between them and the woods. "I thought that was the whole point of my being in deep cover for the FBI."

"It is. It's also the kind of thing that works on a man, maybe makes him take too many chances." He could hear Greer shuffle his feet behind him. "Be careful."

"I am being careful."

"These things can blow up in your face."

Luke's facial muscles tightened automatically as he clenched and unclenched his teeth. "Do you think you have to remind me of that?"

Charles caught his arm. "I'm not sure. Five years ago your fiancée was killed in pursuit of these people and you're still at it."

"That's exactly why I can't quit. Alicia was as dedicated to stopping them as I am."

"Or is it that you don't know anything other than this?" Charles's hand fell away as Luke stared across the darkened room without responding.

The silence hung between them, punctuated by the shrill call of an owl. Luke imagined Charles was replaying that awful night Alicia had died, too. A raid on the Militia that had gone terribly wrong because of a leak inside their department. Now Luke worked alone, except for Greer.

"Enough," Charles said. "I should be keeping us focused on the present."

"Yes, you should."

Charles stood next to him staring at the sky as a cloud passed in front of the moon, obviously trying to get his mind on the work at hand. "Did Bergeron mention this new woman in town?"

Luke's stomach tightened. "What woman?"

"The new vet, did Bergeron mention her or have you seen her with any of his people?"

"No. She helped find the bodies on Swayze's land and from what she said to me I don't think she cares for the Loyalists."

Charles scratched his head and Luke began to feel worried, though he wasn't sure why.

"Keep an eye on her. When she was a teenager her boyfriend was none other than Dubois's son."

Luke's stomach churned. Surely if Jayden had been Militia when she was younger, the Cypress Landing grapevine would have already dropped that bomb on him. But of all people for her to have dated, Mark Dubois would have never crossed his mind.

"I thought Dubois's son died." Luke had only met the head of the local unit a few times. His orders were typically passed on to Luke by Bergeron.

"He died during the bombing of a bank along with the son of a high-profile general and a local girl. I've studied the reports from the incident. They say a girlfriend might have helped, though there's no factual evidence to support the claim, just town gossip. She left right after that and only came back to raise her sister's kids."

Luke waved his hand at Charles to stop him. No doubt the man was talking about Jayden. "I don't see it. Not then and not now."

Charles crossed his arms. "You never know. I said watch her. She comes running home from California to raise her sister's kids then lo and behold, that Walsh guy who lived next to her disappears and at the same time the group takes on a very big, very secretive project. That's a lot of coincidences. We need to stay on top it. There's a reason that reporter is missing. He had to have uncovered important information."

Luke eased out the door. "I'll check into it."

"Don't forget the girl."

Why did everyone think Jayden knew more about Walsh than she was telling? What was he missing? He groaned as he kept moving toward the trees. He didn't bother telling Charles he wouldn't be able to forget the girl for a long time.

JAYDEN SAT IN A BOOTH at Main Street Diner by herself. Two minutes after she'd ordered a sweet tea with lemon, Leigh Fontenot, who was supposed to meet her for lunch, called Jayden's cell to say she'd gotten hung up at work. The restaurant was getting crowded and Jayden began to regret her decision to stay, not that she minded eating by herself. At least she hadn't when she lived in California. But that was the city where no one knew her or spoke to her or wondered why she was by herself. She glanced to the door as she heard it swish open and she nearly strangled on her tea. Luke should have been off modeling for the world's sexiest lawyers calendar in his form-fitting khakis and white shirt. Instead, he was headed straight for her table.

"Mind if I sit with you? It's kind of crowded."

She wondered what he'd say if she told him he was entirely too delicious to sit across from while she tried to eat. The waitress came to take their order and neither one of them spoke until she left.

"You didn't want me to join you."

She narrowed her eyes. She'd have to be more careful if her feelings were that transparent. "I didn't mind. I was meeting Leigh for lunch but she had to cancel, that's what I was thinking."

"Are you sure? Or is it because you're uncomfortable around me since you told me I was good-looking, and I kissed you, and you went through my desk?"

She froze, mouth agape. "I did not say that you were good-looking. Well, I did, but I didn't mean it like that."

"What about the rest?"

Jayden pushed her fork back and forth on the

table. "The rest is true, but it doesn't make me uncomfortable."

He laughed and a few heads turned. She didn't want people speculating. She knew they'd be an item by four this afternoon.

"I do like watching you squirm when I mention your transgressions."

"They're not transgressions."

His eyebrow shot upward.

"Okay, one was a transgression. I don't normally dig into people's desks." She lowered her voice. "You were a part of that kissing thing in case you've forgotten."

He covered her hand in his and her heart rocketed. He tightened his grip when she tried to pull away. "I haven't forgotten, I'll promise you that. It's darned near all I can think of."

Her face flamed and he let her jerk her hand free. "Stop that."

He made a face, exaggeratedly annoyed. "Fine, I'll quit." He tapped his fingers on the table for several seconds before changing the subject. "Did you leave your partner to handle the clinic by himself?"

"We rotate lunch hours. Normally, I eat at the clinic or run home, but like I said, I was supposed to meet Leigh."

"Yeah, I know. She told me to come and fill in for her when she saw she wasn't going to make it."

Jayden wondered why her friend wanted to inflict this torture on her. "How did you see her?"

Once again he gave her a look. "My job does require me to go to the courthouse on occasion. I ran into her in the hall. I was on my way to lunch anyway, and it's bad for your digestion to eat alone."

"What, you're a doctor now, too?"

"Come on, admit it. You didn't like sitting here with half of Cypress Landing wondering why you were eating alone."

She fixed her gaze on the table and played with her napkin before smiling at him. "Okay, you've got me. But now I have to worry about what everyone's thinking when they see me eating with you."

"We'll be the talk of the town."

The waitress brought their food and Jayden didn't bother answering. Instead, she smashed the shrimp po'boy as flat as she could and took a bite.

"I hear you've been the talk of the town before."

She continued chewing as he bit into his own sandwich, but he didn't elaborate. "I don't know what you mean."

He wiped his hands, studying her closely. "I heard you used to date a member of the group you claim to hate so much, that maybe you were involved in a job that killed your boyfriend and two other people."

Three or four shrimp dribbled from the bottom of the sandwich she still held and landed on the plate below. Certain stories never died and she had to admit this one was way too big to disappear, even though she wanted it to.

"That's not how it was." Her voice was weaker than she'd expected, not much more than a whisper. To her dismay her eyes started to burn and her throat tightened. Dragging herself from the booth, she rushed to the restroom—the front door was farther away. She could have sprinted out leaving Luke to pay, although, at the moment, she didn't want him paying for a thing.

The bathroom-stall divider creaked when she leaned against it. She peeled off a piece of tissue and blotted at her eyes. The subject was bound to come up. She hadn't expected Luke to be the first one raising questions and she didn't want to have to delve into her past with him. What would he think?

The time had come to be honest with herself concerning this weakness she was developing for the man. If she admitted she had feelings for him, maybe then she could toss them aside. She had to concentrate on the boys and their needs with no distractions. No other relationships. Not right now, maybe in a year or so when things were settled. If Luke was interested then, well, maybe they'd see what happened. A very high priority was that Luke hear the facts and not a bunch of rumors about her past. After all, he was Elliot's coach and he didn't need to think that one of his players was being raised by a criminal or worse, by a woman who used to be associated with the Loyalists.

At the sink, she dabbed water on her face and nearly laughed. What a lame excuse. Jayden didn't want Luke to have a bad opinion of her. It had nothing to do with boys and everything to do with him.

## CHAPTER TWELVE

WHEN JAYDEN PUSHED open the bathroom door, she imagined that everyone in the diner was staring at her even though she knew it wasn't true. No one knew what Luke had said to her or what she was going to tell him. A story she'd told so many times before she left Cypress Landing, she'd hoped to never tell it again. A brown paper bag sat on their table beside two Styrofoam cups. When he saw her coming Luke got to his feet, picking up the bag and handing her a cup.

"What's this?"

"It's our lunch. I told the waitress I needed to get back to my office."

She frowned.

"We don't have to go to my office, Jayden. I only told her that to cut down on the gossiping about you and I suddenly taking off with our lunch in hand."

"Oh, okay."

She followed him out the door and they started along Main Street in the direction of the courthouse, but a block away, Luke veered down a side street that led to the park. A few other people were enjoying the mild weather and Luke found a picnic table well away from anyone.

He spread his food out and started eating.

"Don't you want me to explain what happened?"

"Not if you don't want to."

Jayden nibbled at her sandwich and debated whether or not to take advantage of the opportunity he'd given her to keep silent. She was surprised to find she wanted to share this with Luke.

"I do."

"Then eat first. You'll be hungry later if you don't."

She tugged at the paper wrapper covering her sandwich expecting that she'd be too upset to eat. But she wasn't. Her stomach rumbled and she took a bite. Had she become so comfortable with Luke that the idea of sharing her past with him didn't bother her?

She finished her last bite and took a long drink of sweet tea. "I was a bit of a hellion when I was a teenager."

Luke feigned surprise. "Not you. And here all this time I thought you were a braniac."

"I was that, too. Straight A's, but I did put my mom through a few trials back then."

"Yourself, too, I guess."

"Yeah, but you don't see it like that when you're young. Everything that goes wrong is always someone else's fault. When I finally grasped that I was making the bed I had to lie in, I straightened up, but it was too late then."

"Does that include joining the Loyalists?"

She shifted on the concrete bench. "It does. Though I never really joined. In the end I was guilty by association."

"What does that mean?" Luke wadded his bag and pushed it aside.

"For my last two years in high school, I dated Mark Dubois."

She noticed the fraction of a pause as Luke lifted his cup to his mouth.

"I see that's a name familiar to you."

"I can't imagine anyone living in this town not recognizing the Dubois name. And we both know I've dealt with members of the Militia."

"Back then Dubois was getting ready to take his place at the head of the Loyalists. But Mark didn't appear to believe in his father's work. He always told me that he wouldn't have any part of it, that he wanted to go to college and be an engineer." She sighed and pushed the hair away from her face. "We talked about leaving Cypress Landing so that he could get away from the pressure his dad put on him to conform to what he wanted." She stopped to watch a couple pass and head for a table at the other side of the park.

"But he finally gave in to Dubois," Luke prompted when she didn't begin immediately.

She drew her attention back to him. "He was lying to me the whole time. Maybe he really did want to be different and he couldn't admit to me that he was doing his father's work." She shrugged. "I went to meetings with him because he said he had to go and I even went to weapons and combat training with him. At first it was fun, and it wasn't as if I supported their cause."

She tapped her finger on the table. The further she went, the harder the story was to tell. But it kept flowing out of her and she didn't want to stop, yet. "It began to get more intense and they wanted me to help them pass out flyers and torment people who went against them. I told Mark I couldn't, and he said we'd leave. But it was a lie. When I wasn't around, he was doing jobs for his father. That's what got him killed."

Luke shifted uncomfortably on the hard bench. So she'd been in love with a boy who lied and led a secret life. For a moment he couldn't look at her. He didn't figure she'd be hoping to repeat the experience.

"What about the Arneaux boy? Was he in the Militia, too?"

She took a napkin from the bag and dabbed at her eyes.

As much as he wanted to know what had happened, he hated seeing her relive the pain. "You can stop if you want."

Jayden shook her head. "No, I'm fine. I thought I'd told this so many times, played it in my head so often, that it wouldn't upset me. But it still does. Louis Arneaux was a good friend, to both Mark and me."

"He was a general's son, right?"

"Louis was named after his dad, Reginald Louis Arneaux, but he always went by his middle name.

His father was in Washington a lot and Louis was supposed to go to West Point, but he didn't want that. We were like the three musketeers that summer. I don't think he joined the Militia. I don't know what happened that evening or who did the planning."

"Did you ever suspect your boyfriend might be lying?"

"Occasionally. My friends, my sister, even my mother tried to tell me I was wrong to believe him. But I figured I knew better than they did."

"When did you finally know the truth?"

"I didn't, don't you see? I believed him right up until he exploded that bomb, killing himself, Louis and the girl in the bank."

Luke went still. This part of Jayden's story sounded like one he'd heard, from another source.

"Who was the girl?"

"The banker's daughter. She earned extra money by cleaning the bank in the evenings after they closed. I guess Mark thought she wouldn't be working so late. I found out later she'd been at cheer-leading practice and had to come after that."

He thumped his hand on the tabletop. "Kent's girlfriend! You remember Kent. He's working in my office this summer. I knew I'd heard this before. Kent had been dating the girl at the bank."

"They'd been best friends and dating for a few years."

She kept her eyes on the table now and Luke figured she was feeling a lot of guilt over that. "That's why it bothered you to see him the other night."

"I'm sure he'll always hold that against me."

"And you had no idea why Dubois was going to the bank?"

"Our friends were having a cookout and that's where we were supposed to go, but we stopped at the bank. I waited in the car while he and Louis went inside." She paused and took a few breaths.

"When they didn't come back right away, I got out and walked toward the door. That's when the building exploded."

She rubbed a long scar that traveled down her bicep. He'd noticed it before.

"You got that then?" He pointed.

"Everything else healed but this was the worst."

"And how did you prove you didn't know anything about what was going on? I mean you'd been dating the guy for a while. I imagine it was hard to get people to believe you."

She gave him a sad smile. "The public defender here at the time was very good."

Luke studied Jayden as she picked up her tea again. Had she not known what was happening? Or, could she have been working with the Militia? He shook off the idea. He played games of deception every day but that didn't mean everyone did.

"See, we public defenders can do good things."

"I never thought you couldn't."

He smiled and reached across the table to take her hand. "That was a long time ago and obviously you couldn't have done anything to stop it."

"Except not be so blinded by my feelings."

"That happens to the best of us."

"Well, I can't let it happen to me again, especially now that I have the boys."

"Is that a warning? You can't get involved because of what could happen?"

She didn't respond but her fingers moved in his hand. Not to pull away but to stroke his palm. His mouth instantly went dry. Did she know she had this effect on him? He finally gripped her hand to stop her.

"Quit that or I'm coming across this table and taking you down on that bench."

Her eyes widened. Nope, she hadn't known. But she did now.

"I think you're a good man, Luke, and I'm not afraid of you."

"You shouldn't be." Inside, he cringed at the lie. But he wanted it to be true. He wanted to protect Jayden from whatever was coming next, and the boys, too. He just had to figure out how to make that happen and still uncover the elusive Militia group he'd been chasing for years. He wasn't sure if that was possible, but he planned to give it the ultimate effort.

"I better get to the clinic."

He nodded and reluctantly let her pull away.

Luke stayed at the bench as Jayden disappeared. He felt another presence behind him before he turned. Speck leaned against a tree a few feet away.

"Looks like you'll be gettin' information from her one way or another, huh? I'll be sure to let the boss know you're more than willing to sweet talk it out of her."

"I'm sure he knows that she'll have to trust me before she'll tell me anything."

Speck snorted and readjusted his dirty ball cap. "Oh, looks like she trusts you all right."

"Did you want something in particular or are you checking up on me?"

"Checking up."

"I'm on my way to my office now. Be sure to add that to your report."

"Will do."

Luke tried not to rush as he left the park, but he was angry. The Militia still felt the need to keep an eye on him. Or maybe that was Speck's idea. They hadn't liked each other from the first meeting, but Luke wasn't in this to make friends with the help. If Bergeron and Dubois trusted him, that was all that mattered. Unfortunately, he couldn't be sure they did.

JAYDEN HEARD RAISED voices before she turned the corner onto Main Street and when she saw who the voices belonged to, her stomach flipped.

"I thought I told you to get rid of that damned dog."

"I am."

Joseph Bergeron caught Amy by the upper arm and shook her until Jayden thought she'd drop the puppy.

"I'm finding him a home, I promise."

"You better or I'll take care of him."

The threat made Jayden sick and she quickened her pace, oblivious to what she might be getting into.

"Amy, have you been to the clinic looking for me?"

The younger woman looked at Jayden, scared but confused.

"I see you've got the dog for me." Jayden turned to Bergeron with a bright smile as if she hadn't heard a word of the previous argument. "Amy came by with it the other day and said she wouldn't be able to keep it. I loved it and told her to give me a day or two to get ready and I'd take it. So I guess you were bringing him to me today, like we arranged."

Jayden held out her hands while Bergeron glanced between the two of them. Amy's face had drained ashen but she handed the puppy over and gave a weak smile. "Yes, I was looking for you. Here he is."

Jayden took the dog, which was shivering slightly, likely scared from the loud voices.

"Thank you so much." She grinned again at Bergeron as if she was overjoyed to finally get the animal.

"Good." The man grunted and stepped off the sidewalk, climbing into his truck.

Amy paused for a fraction of a second then began walking.

"Thanks," she whispered under her breath as she passed Jayden, a tear hanging from her lower lashes.

She wanted to grab Amy and drag her away from this. She hurried to her truck, snuggling the tiny pup under her chin. Oh well, one more warm body at her house couldn't hurt. The boys would be ecstatic. Kasey, however, would not be thrilled.

EVERYONE HAD GONE for the day as Jayden sat at the reception desk completing an order form for supplies and worrying over the day's events with Luke and then with Amy. She heard the knob rattling on the front door and went around the desk into the lobby to unlock it. Amy pushed past her.

"I can only stay a minute. I parked in the back so no one could see me."

"Okay, so what do you need?"

The girl shifted uncomfortably. "Thank you for what you did today. I've held you responsible for my brother's death for a long time. But thank you for taking the dog. Joseph didn't want me to have it in the first place and if you hadn't taken it…"

Jayden sat on a bench in the waiting room and Amy joined her.

"I was happy to. You should have come to me immediately."

"Why would you want to help me?"

"Because you're Mark's sister, and despite what you've been told I loved him and he hid his involvement in the Militia from me. I didn't know what he was doing at the bank. But if I had, I would have tried to talk him out of it."

Amy nodded. "Not all of the Loyalists agreed with what happened that day. I don't know the details. Mark was fighting my father to get out so he could go to college. My dad had promised him if he'd do this one job he'd let him go. I always believed he wanted to leave because of you. At least that's what my father said. I've overheard a few people say my father set the bomb to explode at the wrong time so he would kill Mark. That Mark knew too much about the Militia to be allowed to leave it."

Jayden stared at a black speck on the linoleum. Her eye itched but she couldn't lift her arm let alone blink.

At last, she turned to look at Amy. "Are you telling me all this time I thought Mark was lying, that he was trying to get out?"

Amy nodded and scratched at a hole in her jeans. "That's why I blamed you for his death. If he hadn't wanted to leave with you he might not have died that day." Finally she looked at Jayden. "My brother loved you. He used to talk about you all the time. He would tell me when you and he finished school you'd get married and go away to college. Then I could come live with you and I wouldn't have to be a Militia wife." She focused on the hole in her jeans. "It didn't work out that way."

"Amy, I'm sorry. But just because Mark and I didn't get you out back then doesn't mean you can't get away now. I could give you a little money. You could leave and start a new life."

The other woman shook her head. "He killed my brother for trying to leave. Do you think he'll let me go?"

"You could disappear. I'm sure they haven't let you in on enough for them to care if you left. What could you tell anyone?"

"I've heard plenty. Besides, I've never held a job or managed a bank account. I don't know how to pay bills and keep up with my own money. Except for what I learned in high school, I don't have any skills to get a decent job."

Jayden rubbed her forehead. Amy was right. If she didn't have a clue how to be on her own, she'd be worse off than she was now. Though it was hard to believe anything could be worse.

"We've got to prepare you to get away. Maybe you could take college classes online at the library."

"I'm not sure if I could hide it." Amy sat quietly, scuffing her worn tennis shoe on the floor. "Joseph is gone a lot."

"I'll get information on it. Stop by here again. If anyone asks questions you can say you were checking with me about the puppy."

Amy's eyes clouded. "How is he?"

Jayden smiled and motioned for her to follow. She led her to the counter and pointed behind it where the dog lay curled up in his bed.

"He'll be fine, and the boys will love him. I'll keep him until you can take him back."

"Really?"

"Of course."

"His name is Breeze, because I like to sit on the porch with him in the evening breeze."

"Well, don't worry. Breeze will be fine and if you can sneak away to my house you can come visit him anytime."

She shook her head. "I could never do that." Amy watched the dog a minute. "I've got to go."

"Don't forget to come by and get the school information."

Amy paused at the door. "I might not do it. I have to hide everything and it's hard because I never know who's watching me. Bergeron and my dad have people around that even I don't know about."

She stepped through the door and closed it partially before stopping to stick her head back in. "Be careful looking into that reporter's disappearance, Jayden. I think my dad believes you know more about it than you're telling. That could be dangerous for you."

The door clicked and she was gone. Jayden started gathering her things to go. She had a lot to digest for one afternoon, such as Luke's obvious interest in something more than friendship and her desire to make that happen. Then the bombshell Amy had dropped about Mark. All this time she'd hated him for lying and hated herself for not seeing the truth, when in reality, Mark's love for her had been true. He'd been trying to leave his father behind and make a life with her. She sighed and gathered up the puppy. If it was true that Paul Dubois had killed his own son for wanting to leave, what would he do to her if he thought she had information he wanted? She locked the office door.

When she pulled into her mother's drive to pick up Garrett and Elliot, she knew the events of ten years ago would always hang over her. She got out of her truck and eyed the shiny Mercedes parked near the front steps. General Reginald Arneaux was here and if the relationship between him and her mother became permanent she'd have a constant reminder of the best friend she'd let die because she was ignorant of what was going on around her.

## CHAPTER THIRTEEN

JAYDEN FINGERED THE yellow tape across the front of the small porch, then ducked under it and climbed the steps. She was probably breaking a law again, but she did own the place. If she wanted to go inside and see the damage done by the sheriff and his men during their search, she should be able to.

Turning the key in the lock, Jayden put aside her rationalizations. Paul Dubois thought she knew something that could incriminate the Loyalists. She didn't, but maybe she was missing a clue right here in front of her. She wandered from room to room, stepping over the contents of several drawers that the officers had dumped on the floor and making a point not to touch anything.

*What happened to you, Eric?* He'd been working on an angle he thought was very important. That much she knew. Now she wished she'd taken more time to talk with him, but those first weeks she'd been here after the loss of her sister had been excruciating, and she'd had no time to spend with a stranger renting the house beside her.

"Aunt J., are you in here?"

Jayden spun around and hurried to the front of the house where Elliot waited half a step inside.

"I don't think you're supposed to be in here, Aunt J."

"You're right. I only wanted to see what kind of mess the sheriff and his men left so I'd know how much we've got to clean up."

"Oh, I thought you might be looking to see if you could find a clue that the sheriff missed."

She stared at the boy as he glanced around the room. He was too smart for his own good.

"Well, maybe I was doing that, too."

"I keep trying to remember things Eric said that would help, but I can't think of anything. He threw the ball with me and that's mostly what we talked about."

She nodded as they stepped outside and she locked the door.

"Why do you think the Militia wanted to get rid of Mr. Eric?" he asked.

"We don't know for sure it was them. We only suspect it could be. Besides, we don't know what happened to Eric yet."

"Do you think they'll want to get rid of us, too?"

She hugged him to her. "Elliot, for heaven's sake, no, I don't. We suspect them in Eric's disappearance because he was a reporter doing a story on them and it wouldn't be a nice one. He was going to expose a lot of things they do that are illegal. That's why we think they might have wanted him stopped."

"What if they think he told us what he'd found?"

Elliot could figure things out much more quickly than she could. Unless…

"Has someone been asking you questions about what Eric might have said to you?"

The boy shook his head and she drew a relieved breath. She didn't need him worrying about dangers that might never materialize.

"They know we'd tell the police if we knew anything."

Elliot was quiet as he walked beside her on the path back to their house.

"What if we didn't? What if they thought we weren't telling the police for a reason?"

She stopped in her tracks and caught him by the wrist, pulling him around to face her.

"What is that supposed to mean? Have you not told the police everything?"

"I've told them all I know for sure, but one time I heard Eric say that the Loyalists had infitted…" he paused and shook his head "…infillaped, no, that wasn't it."

"Do you mean infiltrated?"

"Yeah, that was what he said. They had infiltrated the police and the sheriff's office and the courts."

The hair on the back of Jayden's neck tingled and for a moment she almost felt as though they were being watched. She glanced toward her mother's small hair salon and saw movement in the window. That's likely all it was, her mother had looked out at them.

"What did he mean by that, Aunt J., infiltrated? And Mr. Luke is in the court system, isn't he?"

"It means he thought people who work for the sheriff are also with the Militia."

"Does that mean he thought Mr. Luke was in the Militia?"

"I don't think so. Besides, Eric was guessing. He didn't know anything for certain. That's only what he thought."

"Mr. Luke did help that man not go to jail. The one who was driving the car that killed Mom and Dad. That guy was one of them."

"That's true, Elliot, but he got that case because he's the public defender and was appointed to take it since the man didn't have money for his own lawyer. It's the way the legal system works. Do you think Luke is helping those people?"

"No, not really. I like him and I don't think he'd do wrong. It's hard to see Mr. Luke working with that guy, though, even if he had to."

"Do you hold that against Mr. Luke or does it make you feel mad at him?"

"No. Gran has always said the same thing as you. He didn't get to pick the people he has to help in court. But I think if he had a family and a wife he might not want to do that kind of stuff anymore."

She stared at Elliot then started toward the house again. She wasn't at all sure where this was coming from, or worse, where it was going. Was Elliot matchmaking?

"Don't you think a man as nice as Mr. Luke should have a family?"

"I guess so, Elliot."

"He'd probably be an awesome dad, huh?"

"I don't know. Maybe."

"Do you think you'll every marry Mr. Luke?"

She stopped mid-stride and gaped at him. "What is this, the Spanish Inquisition?"

Elliot frowned. "What's that?"

Jayden rubbed her forehead and started walking again. "Oh, never mind. Why would you ask me if I'll ever marry Luke? We don't even date."

"But you went with him that day on the boat when we fished."

"I didn't know Mr. Luke well enough to let you go off with him alone."

"Oh." He seemed to worry that thought in his mind before continuing. "You could still date him if you wanted. I think he likes you."

"I'm not concerned whether Luke likes me or not. I want to make sure you and Garrett are safe and that you have the things you need."

"But Mr. Luke is good with kids and he likes me and Garrett."

Jayden's insides were starting to hurt already. Luke was good with kids. Meaning what? She wasn't? Of course, she didn't know what she was doing. She probably made a million mistakes and the boys likely went to bed wondering why their mother had left them to someone so clueless. She knotted her hands into fists to stop them from shaking, but that only made her eyes start burning and she prayed she wouldn't break down and cry. What was she doing here? She'd made horrible mistakes in the past. Why would anyone think she could do better with these two boys?

"Aunt J., don't you think if you married Mr. Luke, it would be cool? We could all live together and he could help you."

They'd finally made it to the bottom of the steps and Jayden stopped. Her throat tightened and, to her horror, tears spilled over onto her cheeks.

"What is this, Elliot? Why are you trying to marry me off to Luke? Is it so terrible, just the three of us with Gran right next door? Am I doing a bad job since I came here? I know I've never had children of my own, so I don't know exactly what I'm doing, but has it been so awful? No one's gotten hurt. You get to play the sports you want. What am I not doing right?"

He looked at her, his lower lip trembling slightly, and she wanted to kick herself, except that her own lip was trembling. She hadn't asked for this mothering job and she'd never promised to be good at it. Did the boys think she needed Luke to help her?

"I was only thinking about you, Aunt J. I want you to be happy here." He turned and ran up the steps, slamming the door behind him. She dropped onto the porch, her head on her knees. She was completely losing it. Sure, Elliot thought getting her a husband would keep her happy and keep her here. He'd seen his mother and his father as a happy couple so he automatically thought she'd be happier with a man in her life.

The sound of tires crunching on the gravel drive made her lift her head, but she immediately dropped it back to her knees. Great, Luke, the exact person she didn't want to see. The floodgates had been opened and she couldn't seem to quit crying. Luke would have to deal with her being upset or leave.

His legs bumped against hers as he sat on the step. A soothing hand stroked her back. "What's wrong, Jayden?"

She hugged her knees to her chest. "I'm not cut out to be a parent."

"You're doing fine. Why wouldn't you think so?"

"Because I went nuts with Elliot after he'd spent five minutes trying to tell me why it would be great if you and I were married."

She felt rather than heard him chuckle and she jerked her tear-streaked face to him. "It's not funny!"

"I'm not laughing. I kind of like his way of thinking. Why did it upset you so much? Except for the obvious, which is that he's trying to marry us off and we're not even dating."

"I felt like he was trying to tell me I needed help, that I wasn't doing an adequate job."

"Jayden, he's ten. I doubt he'd be that subtle. If he thought you were screwing up I imagine he'd come right out and say so."

"I know that, but I completely lost it anyway. I yelled at him."

Luke wiped her tears and pushed the hair away from her face. "Everybody loses it—parents, kids, aunts, boyfriends."

Suddenly she felt exhausted and without thinking leaned against Luke, grateful for his strength.

"He doesn't deserve this from me, not after all that's happened. But I'm constantly scared that I'm going to make a mistake, mess up, not be the parent they need me to be. I felt as if he thought I was coming up short."

"That sounds like your thinking, not his." Luke shifted on the step to put his arms around her. "Jayden, I've never been a parent, either, but I'm certain some or all of those things will definitely happen. And the three of you will survive it."

"Because that's what makes us a family, right?"

"I'm pretty sure that's how it goes. Why don't you go talk to him?"

She wiped her palms over her face and stood. Now she had to go fix this with Elliot. He had to know that her happiness didn't depend on a man, although she sure felt a lot better right now because of Luke.

She found Elliot sitting on his bed and he hastily wiped his face when she came in. She'd been doing the same thing on her way down the hall.

"Hey." Jayden sat on the bed beside him.

"Hey." Elliot stared at his knees, picking at the bedspread.

"I'm sorry, Elliot. I acted like a dummy a minute ago. I'm always scared I'm not doing what your mom would have done and I imagined for a minute you thought I needed help."

"That's not what I meant."

"I see that now. But I said all that stuff without thinking. I was in a panic."

"Why would you be in a panic?"

"I don't want you or your brother to miss out on anything or be unhappy because I'm doing the wrong thing."

He titled his head to one side, his eyes narrowing. "Why would you be doing the wrong thing?"

"I've never been a mom before and, while I know I'll never replace your mother, I want to try and be as great at the mom job as she was."

"But you are great."

She smiled and pulled him close. "Are you saying that to be nice to me?"

Elliot put both arms around her waist and hugged her. "It's true."

"So we don't need Mr. Taylor to hold things together, do we?"

"No, but I still think he likes you."

She hugged Elliot closer, not wanting him to see her face, which might tell him she was beginning to like Mr. Taylor, too.

"For now we should all stay friends. What do you think?"

"I think that's fine."

"Let's see what we can make for dinner."

"I want fried chicken. We haven't had that in a long time."

"Fried chicken it is, then." She got to her feet to follow Elliot who'd already started toward the kitchen. "Oh, by the way, Mr. Luke will be having dinner with us."

The boy turned, looking even more confused.

She shrugged. "He showed up a few minutes ago. I didn't invite him over."

"I told you he likes you." Elliot trotted ahead to find Luke.

## CHAPTER FOURTEEN

"WE'RE RUNNING LOW on hot dogs and hamburgers."

Jayden glanced at Leigh and frowned. The local Little League teams were hosting an all-day baseball tournament, and luckily for her it wasn't her Saturday to work at the clinic. At the moment, though, she didn't feel too lucky.

Leigh was still standing in the concession stand holding a half-empty box of hot dogs.

"What do you want me to do about it?"

"Go tell Luke. He was responsible for getting the food."

"You go tell him."

"Can you not see that I'm in the middle of something?"

Jayden eyed the box Leigh was waggling and the customer at the counter. Grumbling to herself, she tossed the paper towel she held into the garbage and left the small block building in search of Luke.

"And a few more cases of soda, too!" Leigh shouted after her.

Nearly ten minutes later, she found him working on the faucet in one of the bathroom facilities with a wrench. His baseball cap shadowed his face and, even though it was cool, sweat trickled down his cheek. She leaned against the doorway, watching him.

"Did they teach plumbing in law school?"

He glanced her way and grinned. At the simple action, Jayden found herself giddy. Luke was an attractive man, so maybe anyone would get butterflies at the sight of his electric smile. He gave the pipe one last turn and stood.

He stopped in front of her and slipped his arm around her waist, pulling her closer. "I had a number of jobs to help pay for law school and construction was one of them."

He added more pressure at her waist until she was leaning against him and she had to move her feet or fall over. When she stepped forward a half inch, their bodies met from thigh to waist and she leaned back to see his face. People wandered by and she knew she should be more concerned about the image she was presenting standing in the door of the bathroom in the grip of one of the town's most eligible and elusive bachelors, but she couldn't seem to care. Being in Luke's arms felt the same as coming home to Cypress Landing—a little scary but exactly where she belonged.

"You're not trying to get away."

"No, I'm not. Should I be?"

He shook his head. "I'm hoping you'll want to get closer."

"That sounds interesting."

"Well, that makes my day." He lowered his head to brush his lips against hers.

"Luke, people are watching us. You'll have the rumor mill rolling now."

"Damn the rumor mill. It's not a rumor if it's true. I truly wanted to kiss you and I want to do it much more."

"Hopefully, not in public."

"No, you're right. Private would be much better, preferably not in a bathroom."

"Yeah, this bathroom isn't so great and I think there are people waiting to get in. I did come looking for you for a reason."

He groaned. "I should have known. What is it?"

"Leigh says we're running out of soda and hot dogs."

"Oh, is that all? No problem there. The rest are at my house. We didn't have room in the coolers."

He bent to capture her lips once more then caught her hand, pulling her along behind him.

"Come on. You and Kent can go and get them."

Her steps slowed, dragging Luke's shoulder backward.

"What's wrong?"

"I was working in concessions."

"They'll survive without you."

Jayden still hesitated. "You and I could go or I can go by myself."

"As much as I like the idea of getting you alone at my house, I can't do it. I've got to get the team together and get them warmed up because we play in less than an hour. The drink cases and those big boxes of hot dogs are heavy. You shouldn't try to load them by yourself." He paused for a moment, then started walking again, pulling her along with him. "I guess Kent can go alone but it would be better if he had help. If you don't want to go— Wait, this is about something else, isn't it?"

He stopped and turned to face her. "Kent doesn't hold that against you."

"Of course he does."

"Okay, so maybe he does. He works with me, Jayden, and he and I are together a lot. You're going to have to be around him sooner or later."

"I haven't seen him around you lately."

"That's because he was gone to visit his mother. But he's back now and you need to resolve this. It's one more thing you can feel better about when you set the story straight with him. Tell him what happened."

"I'm sure he's heard it before."

"But not from you."

She nodded. "What if he doesn't want to hear?"

"He's a good guy. He'll listen."

Luke led her straight toward the person in Cypress Landing who possibly hated her the most, Kent Raynor.

She fidgeted in her seat as Kent drove to Luke's house. He hadn't been the least bit happy about going on this errand with her, but he'd done it without argument, which was more than she could say for herself. Sitting here in silence wasn't helping her nerves.

She had to start somewhere. "Go ahead and say whatever you'd like to say."

She noticed his fingers tighten on the wheel. "I don't have anything to say to you." He stared intently at the road, but she could see the muscles in his face tightening.

"I'd like to tell you my side of the story."

They'd come to a stop sign and Kent shook his head. Then he gunned the engine, the force jerking her backward against the seat. "That's all it would be, Jayden, a story."

"Kent, I know you're mad about what happened."

"Mad? You think I'm mad?" He shot her an angry look before turning his attention back to the road. "You killed my girlfriend when she was only sixteen years old. We had plans to get married when we finished school."

Jayden thought he'd finished, but when he spoke again, his words came out slower and more pained than angry. "It took me years of jumping from school to school, partying my ass off and working odd jobs to pay for tuition and alcohol before I finally saw that I wasn't only hurting myself but Megan's memory. I knew she wouldn't have wanted that for me. Not to mention what I was doing to my mom, who'd been through enough in her own life."

He stopped and she rubbed at a mustard spot on her shorts.

"How is your mom? I always admired her for going to school and becoming a nurse. She worked hard."

"Yes, she did. After I graduated she got married again, a lawyer, but they moved away from here a few years ago. He's the one who helped me get my life back on track and get into law school."

"Who did she marry?"

He turned into Luke's drive and parked before he looked at her. "The lawyer who got you off for killing my girlfriend, Megan."

He got out of the truck, but she was right behind him. "Then you should know that I had no idea what was happening that night."

"So you and my stepdad say."

She touched his arm, but he shook her off. "It's true, Kent. I didn't know Mark was in the Militia and I certainly didn't know he was doing jobs for them—like bombing banks. He kept telling me he wasn't part of it. I think he didn't want to be, but his father kept forcing him."

"So he forced you to participate, too."

"That's not true. We were going to a friend's house that night. I didn't know why he stopped at the bank. He always said we'd leave here when we got out of school so he could get away from his dad."

"His father wasn't letting him go anywhere, Jayden. I'm sure he knew that. He'd probably have killed him first."

"Yeah, you're right. He would."

Kent paused in the middle of stacking boxes from the refrigerator on the floor. "What are you saying?"

"You know exactly what I'm saying. I believe his father set him up to die and that Megan Johnson got in the way. He may have intended for me to be inside the bank, too."

Kent was still bent over the boxes. "It nearly destroyed me to lose her."

Jayden sighed and he straightened to face her.

"Kent, I lost people I loved in that explosion, too. Mark and I had planned our future, and Louis was going to leave and go to school. If I'd known what was happening I'd have tried to stop it, but I didn't. I don't believe Mark knew Megan was there."

"She wasn't supposed to be. She was later than normal getting finished."

"I carry the guilt of their deaths every day. I was listening to the radio and didn't want to go with them to make an after-hours deposit, which is what Mark said they were doing."

Kent shut the refrigerator and she picked up two boxes while he grabbed the rest. "This should be enough and if not we can come back for more."

She nodded and led the way to the truck. As she slid her load onto the backseat, Kent did the same on the other side.

"I never considered how you might feel if you didn't know what was going on that night. I guess I wanted to make you guilty. Mark and Louis were dead. It was easier to hate you because you were alive."

"Me and Mark's dad."

"I never thought about Mark's dad being involved. Not in that way. But it makes sense. I grew up in that atmosphere, with my real dad in the Militia. I know the pressure to conform and there's no easy way to escape."

They climbed into the truck and started back to the baseball diamond. Kent questioned her about her years in vet school and about California. Another weight lifted from Jayden's shoulders. This one she owed to Luke.

LEAPING FROM HER CHAIR, Jayden cheered in the winning run. Elliot's team had squeaked by with a one-run win, and the boys gathered in the field to shake hands with the opposing team.

Elliot came running to her when they were finished. "Did you see that, Aunt J.? We won on Steven's hit."

"I know. All that batting practice you guys have been doing paid off, didn't it?"

"Sure did."

Luke jogged up to them with Garrett on his back. "Great game, Coach."

He smiled at her, sliding Garrett to the ground. He pulled his wallet from his pocket and before she knew what he was doing he handed Elliot several bills. "You two go get a hot dog or hamburger. We'll catch up in a minute."

Garrett's eyes bulged at the sight of the money, but Elliot took it calmly, as though his coach bought him food every day.

"Thanks, Mr. Luke." He turned and hurried away before Jayden could stop him.

"Don't argue over who gets what!" Luke shouted after them.

"We won't," they answered in unison then kept going.

"But, of course, they will."

He laughed. "I don't doubt it."

"You didn't have to do that. I have money for them to buy food."

"It's no big deal. As bad as it sounds, I was trying to get rid of them so I could talk to you alone."

She glanced at the throng of people around them. "Yeah, like that's going to happen."

He surveyed the ballpark then started walking. After several steps he turned back. "Are you coming?"

With long strides she caught up to him and didn't bother to ask where they were going. In a few minutes it became apparent that they were headed for his truck. Pressing the automatic lock on the keys, he opened the door for her. She stepped in feeling much like a teenager sneaking away. Luke slid in on the other side and started the engine, turning the air-conditioning on low.

He faced her and smiled wryly. "Sorry, this was all I could think of."

"You could have waited until another time."

"I didn't want to. Did you?" He leaned closer.

"Not really. I feel like a kid." Jayden glanced through the front windshield toward the field. They were far enough away to feel like they had privacy, sort of.

"Me, too, though it's not such a bad thing, wanting to be alone with each other for a minute."

"No, it's not."

"How did it go with Kent?"

"It went well. Thank you for making me do what I probably would never have on my own."

"You'd have gotten around to it."

She traced a pattern on the dash. "I don't think so. I would have worried about it forever, I guess."

He reached across and took her hand in his. "Then I'm glad I talked you into going."

They sat staring at each other until Jayden couldn't stand it any longer and she pushed forward on her knees, falling against Luke. Her mouth caught his in a hungry kiss. His gasp told her he hadn't been expecting her attack, but then neither had she. When his lips parted under her pressure she also knew he didn't mind. He pulled her onto his lap and she forgot to worry whether they could be seen. His hands traveled along her side to the edge of her T-shirt, fingering their way underneath. When his fingertips touched her bare skin she shivered and when his palm covered her breast she couldn't suppress a moan. Luke answered by deepening his kiss then moving to kiss her jawline, her neck and the edge of her T-shirt. He pushed her away gently, his hand still smoothing the lacy fabric separating his palm from her skin.

"Jayden, this is crazy."

She nodded and licked her lips. They felt swollen.

Luke rested his forehead against her. "But every minute I'm with you, you amaze me and I want more. I want you."

She shook her head. "We can't make out in this truck in the middle of the ball game."

He reluctantly slipped his hand from her shirt. "You're right. I got carried away."

"I believe I was first."

His lips twitched. "You were, weren't you?"

She leaned toward him again and he put his hands on her.

"What are you doing?"

"I said we didn't need to make out in here. That doesn't mean I can't kiss you again."

He slid one hand from her shoulder to the back of her neck, pulling her to his mouth. It was her destination anyway. As his breath fanned her face, he held away from her for a few seconds, not touching, both taking in the very breath of each other. At that moment, she recognized she loved Luke. The last man on earth she would have expected to love. He'd turned out to be everything she might ever have dreamed of, which was frightening. A man who resembled a dream come true might become a nightmare. When Luke finally closed the distance between them, she experienced the same feelings she had earlier today—safety, warmth. How could that not be true?

With Jayden next to him, Luke could forget about revenge, which he'd found didn't taste nearly as sweet as the woman he held. She was a magnificent combination of strength, beauty and passion that made him want to back this truck out and drive away with her. No, check that, it made him want to go snatch those two boys and drive away with the crew of them, and maybe even pick up her mother along the way. If this was what it meant to have a family, he was all in.

He heard a thump behind his head. He ignored it and tried to pull Jayden closer, but she pushed him away.

"Luke, someone's at the door."

"It's Pete. Ignore him. He'll go away."

"Don't be silly, we can't."

He groaned and slid Jayden to the other side of the truck then rolled down the window. "What?"

Pete wore a huge grin while trying to look serious. "Sorry, but we need you to help with the brackets for the final games and there's a mom waiting for Jayden to relieve her in the concession stand so she can see her son play."

"Fine, we're coming."

He raised the window and looked back as he reached for the door. "I'll go ahead. Lock the truck when you get out, okay."

"All right."

He watched her run her fingers through her hair as he clutched the door handle. "Oh, and, Jayden?"

"Yeah?"

"When I said this was crazy, what I meant was that I'm crazy about you."

He loved the stunned expression on her face. She hadn't expected that from him. It was so completely out of character that he was surprised himself. Though, he now knew it had been brewing inside of him for days.

He hit the ground at a brisk walk until he caught up to Pete. "Don't say a word."

"I wasn't going to say anything at all. Not I told you so or I knew it would work. Nothing like that."

Luke cursed under his breath, and Pete laughed. "You're too uptight. Except for a minute ago when you seemed very loose. I think Jayden Miller might be good for you."

"I don't want a lot of gossip racing all over town."

"Well, maybe you should have thought of that before you kissed her in the door of the bathroom, and then huddled in your truck steaming the windows."

"We did not steam the windows."

"Might as well have."

"And how did you know about the bathroom?"

"Leigh saw you from the concession stand, along with half the single women who've been trying to get to that point with you for two years."

"So the proverbial cat's out of the bag."

"Oh, yeah, I'll say. All those boys ever talk about is Mr. Luke this, and Mr. Luke that. They're both all for you."

"You think they'd like having me around?"

"I know they would. Are you planning on being around?"

He slowed as they approached the tent where they were preparing the posters for the final games. "I think I might, Pete. I really do."

The other man laughed. "You say it like you're scared to death, Taylor. It's not a bad thing."

"I don't know how to be a family man."

Pete crossed his arms. "You're serious, aren't you?"

"Beyond serious."

"You'll do fine. Go with your instincts. That always seems to work for me."

Luke started toward the tent wondering what kind of instincts he had. Being with Jayden and the boys long-term would be so difficult he tried not to line up all the events that would have to take place to make it happen. He knew how unattainable it was. He preferred to push the thought away and, for one evening, concentrate on the possibilities.

ONE THING LUKE HADN'T BEEN prepared for was the fallout from his declaration that he was ready to start dating now. If anything, he'd have expected the other women to give Jayden dirty looks, not wage a full-force advance on him. He'd been hit on no less than three times this evening. Couldn't they see he was only interested in one woman? And now he found himself cornered at the tailgate of his truck by Karen Singley.

"I've heard that you're ready to leave your celibate days behind."

"What celibate days?"

"The ones you said you were living after the death of your fiancée. That was your reason for not going skinny-dipping in your pool with me, remember?"

Had he said that? He might have said anything to get this woman off his back.

"Oh, those. Well, I've met someone who's special to me. I want to spend time with her."

"You should shop around, Luke, now that you're putting yourself back on the market."

"I'm not on the market." She made him sound like a side of beef.

"You're honestly seeing that Miller girl, exclusively?"

"Looks that way."

"That's too bad. At the first sign of trouble she's likely to up and run off again."

Luke gritted his teeth. "I'm not worried."

"If you change your mind…" she shrugged and leaned forward so her low-cut shirt gave him a full view of her breasts, which were pushed up and barely covered by a black bra "…I'll be around."

"I won't change my mind," he stated firmly as she walked away. He tossed the last bag of baseballs in his truck bed then scanned the parking lot for Jayden's SUV. He spotted her several cars away helping Garrett get his seat belt fastened. The tournament had finally ended at ten o'clock, and after a full day both boys were already half asleep.

Making use of his long legs, he caught her as she reached for her door. He wanted to touch her, but he could see Elliot eyeing them through the window. Instead, she reached toward him, catching his fingers in hers.

"Congratulations, Coach. Second place in this tournament is an honor."

He grinned. "Yep, that was one of the top teams in the state that took first."

"So I heard."

He moved to one side, leaning against the truck. He let his hand glide up her arm then back to her fingers.

"This has been a terrific day for me, Jayden."

"For me, too. I'm beginning to feel at home again here. I was afraid I never would."

"Me, too."

She gave an unladylike snort. "You're practically homegrown, Luke. Or at least everyone thinks so."

"Everyone but me. Today I felt it or maybe I was feeling something else I liked just as much."

She moved a step closer to him. "Did you mean it when you said you were crazy about me?"

He chuckled. "You better believe I meant it."

"Good, because I'm afraid I've gone a bit crazy for you, too."

He closed the distance between them, stopping with his lips inches from hers. "Only a bit?"

"Quite a lot actually. Almost insanely crazy."

He kissed her and had to force himself to break away. Squeezing her hand, he brought it to his lips. "Be careful going home. I'll be thinking about you." He rushed back to his own truck before he could change his mind and climb in the SUV with her and the boys. At the moment he didn't care if he had to sleep on the couch. If he could be in the same house with them he'd be happy.

The door had barely slammed behind her when Elliot started.

"I saw Mr. Luke kiss you."

She decided to deal with the questions rather than try to change the subject. "Yes, you did. Is that okay?"

"It is if you wanted him to, but if you didn't I'd be mad."

"No, I wanted him to."

"Okay." He was quiet for a few seconds. "That's kind of gross, Aunt J."

She laughed. "Maybe you won't think so when you get a little older."

From the lack of input on Garrett's part she could only assume he was asleep, thank goodness. She didn't know if she could handle both of them quizzing her at the same time.

"Does this mean you're not just friends with Mr. Luke anymore?"

"I guess it does."

"Cool."

Obviously, that meant all was well in Elliot's world.

At home she parked under the attached carport and pulled Garrett from his seat. He'd soon be too heavy for her to carry. Halfway across the walkway to the kitchen door she noticed a pool of water in the yard.

"Oh, no."

"What is it?"

"Garrett must have left on the water hose. It's made a pond in the yard."

She gave Garrett a gentle shake. "You've got to get down so I can go turn the hose off."

He struggled to his feet and she hurried to the spigot, feeling the mud ooze into her shoes.

When she made it back to the sidewalk, she kicked off her shoes and grimaced. Now was not the time to fuss about the water. They were all too tired. She'd have a talk with Garrett about it tomorrow. The motion detector that controlled the sidewalk light must have broken because they were still standing in the dark.

"Elliot, go back in the garage and turn on the lights out here."

She had one foot on the step to the kitchen door when the lights flashed on. The large, muddy footprint ahead of hers caught her attention first, then the splintered wood of the door frame. She backed away slowly, pulling Garrett with her.

"Get back in the car, Elliot."

"What?"

"Do as I say. Get in the car now."

She jerked Garrett into her arms and ran to her vehicle, slamming and locking the doors behind them. Driving with one hand, she dialed her cell phone with the other. The dispatcher's voice came over the line.

"Yes, I'd like to report a possible break-in at my house."

"A break-in, Aunt J.! What are you talking about?"

"Shh."

She gave her address to the operator who'd taken her call.

Spinning into her mother's drive, she hit her number on speed dial.

"Get up," she said when her mom answered. "We need to get in your house."

In front of her the lights came on and her mother appeared on the porch, along with Kasey and Breeze, who'd spent the day with her while they were at the ball game.

"What's going on, Jayden?"

Pulling the two boys up the steps, she raced inside.

"Someone's been in my house."

## CHAPTER FIFTEEN

"ARE YOU SURE YOU don't see anything missing?"

Jayden nodded as Jackson Cooper led her back to the front porch. The sheriff's men had secured the scene and gone through her house, carefully collecting possible evidence and checking for fingerprints. Someone had turned the place upside down—several of the interior doors were broken, as well as the one where the intruder had entered.

When she got to the bottom of the steps, Luke materialized beside her and put his arms around her. He'd been her support all night.

"Thanks for coming and hanging around."

"I wanted to be here."

She pulled away, noticing that Jackson had followed her. "If you'll leave us a key, Ms. Miller, we'll lock the house when we leave and you can go. We've fixed the door as best we could. It should hold until you can get someone in here to do it properly. We'll probably be back tomorrow for more evidence, then we'll be able to let you back in. Do you have a place to stay?"

"Yeah, with my mom." She glanced at her watch.

"Oh, no, it's two in the morning and I just remembered she's leaving on a trip later today. I've got to get back there so she can get some sleep." She pulled a key from her ring and handed it to Jackson. "I'll get this back from you tomorrow."

He nodded, and she hurried to her car. When she opened the door Luke said, "I'm following you in my truck."

As she pulled away, she saw Pete stop him. She was glad he'd been there. Even with all the officers on the scene, she hadn't felt truly safe until Luke held her. On the short trip to her mom's she tried to convince herself she'd be able to stay in the house again and not be afraid. Who would break into her house and not steal things? She didn't want to imagine that it might have to do with Eric Walsh, but she couldn't think of another reason.

Her mother must have been watching for her, because she opened the door as Jayden climbed the steps to the front porch.

"What did they find?"

"Nothing."

"What do you mean nothing?"

"My house is a wreck but they haven't found fingerprints yet and nothing's been taken as far as I can tell. Even the muddy prints had been wiped clean in the house. They must have missed the one on the step."

"It's a good thing you saw it."

Jayden sank into a chair at the kitchen table.

"Was someone else coming here?" Her mother

stared through the window at the approaching headlights.

"Oh, yeah, that's Luke. Where are the boys?"

"I put them in my bed for now. They can sleep there tonight." Her mother went to let Luke in. Jayden traced her finger along the wood grain of the table.

"I told Jayden they could stay here with me." She heard her mother's voice from the other room.

"But aren't you leaving in a few hours on that cruise with your girlfriends?"

"I can't go and leave Jayden and the boys now."

When Jayden realized they intended on having a discussion without any input from her, she got to her feet to join them.

"Yes, you can."

They both turned to look at her. "You're going on that trip, Mom, and we can stay here in your house. We'll be fine."

"No," Luke and her mother said in unison, glancing at each other.

Luke came over and took her hand. "You can't stay here. Your mother doesn't have an alarm system."

"That's silly. I don't have an alarm system in my house."

"That's about to change. You and the boys stay with me until I can call in a favor and get a security system installed."

"That's a nice offer, Luke, but we can't do that. What would people think?"

"They'd think I was helping my girlfriend."

"I'm not your girlfriend."

"Yes, you are. Or do you kiss every guy off the street like you did me tonight?"

Jayden could feel her face getting red as she tried to ignore her mother's arched eyebrows. But the woman wouldn't be ignored. "Jayden, quit worrying so much about what people think and do what you need to do. The only way I'll go on this trip is if you stay with Luke."

"That's blackmail, Mom."

"What's your point?"

She weighed her options. Her mother had been looking forward to this trip for months.

"Fine, we'll stay at your house."

He took her hand in his. "Now you're making sense. So both of you get your things and the boys. We'll come back to your house in the morning for more clothes."

Evette frowned. "Wait, not both of us. I'm not going with you."

Luke released Jayden to face her mother. "You don't think I'm letting you stay here alone after they broke into Jayden's house, do you?"

"But didn't you hear Jayden? I'm leaving in only a few hours. I have to get up and meet my friends for the drive to New Orleans."

"You'll spend those hours at my house. We can all have a cup of coffee before you go."

Her mother rolled her eyes and stomped down the hall. Jayden grinned at Luke. "Thank you. I didn't want her to stay here alone either, not even for a few minutes." He followed her to her mother's bedroom and helped Jayden move the boys to the car.

JAYDEN SNUGGLED UNDER the covers in Luke's huge king-size bed, glad that he'd won the argument about where everyone should sleep. He'd put her mother and the boys in the two guest rooms and taken the couch for himself, even though she'd tried to insist she should be the one on the couch. He'd ignored her and all but carried her to his room. "Now stay there and don't come out until I say so," he'd ordered. When she climbed between the sheets, exhaustion overtook her. She imagined Luke was tired, too, but she heard him get the boys off to bed as well as her mother, who he promised to wake up in time for her trip. The house grew quiet around her, but when the door opened she sat up.

"Sorry, but Pete's phone call caught me right before I got in the shower and I truly need one."

"That's fine."

He hesitated for a moment then hurried into the adjoining bathroom. When she heard water running she contemplated slipping in to join him, but decided against it. Besides, they were both exhausted.

When the bathroom door opened, Jayden jerked awake, surprised she'd been able to doze off. "Luke?"

"Yeah?"

"Would you come and lie here for a minute?"

She felt the bed move under his weight as he slid next to her, pulling a throw on top of him.

"Don't you want to get under the cover?"

He rolled her on one side so her back was to him then he pulled her closer. "That would be way too much temptation for one man with your mother and two little boys right down the hall."

"I see your point."

Neither spoke as he kissed the back of her neck then rested against the pillow. She would never have felt safe at her mom's house, but here, in Luke's arms, she felt more protected than she ever had in her life.

"Do you think the break-in was connected to Eric?"

He slid his hand up and down her side.

"Luke?"

"I don't know what to say, Jayden. I guess, yeah, I do think it could be about that. Did Walsh leave anything with you? A notebook, a memory stick, digital recorder—anything at all?"

"No. We didn't even talk much about what he was working on. Or at least he didn't tell me. We discussed the town and the Militia in general, but nothing specific. He certainly never hinted that he might be in danger."

Luke tightened his hold on her. "Don't worry. You'll be safe here and I'll take care of your house."

"You don't have to worry about my house."

"Jayden, would you, this once, let me help you without an argument?"

"Maybe."

"Good, now let's get some sleep. The alarm on my

watch is set for six a.m. I promised your mother I'd have coffee ready before she had to leave."

Jayden snuggled deeper into the mattress. Within seconds she heard Luke's steady breathing. This was a man she could trust. She closed her eyes and slept.

IT HAD BEEN AN unusual week staying at Luke's house. Jayden had thought she'd feel uncomfortable or strange, when in fact, they all fell easily into a routine. All week, Steven's teenage babysitter had also picked up Elliot and Garrett. The girl stayed with them at the Fontenot's house until either she or Luke could get them. Today, as she parked her car in their driveway, she could see that Leigh was already home.

She opened the side door as she knocked and entered the kitchen. Huge pizza boxes lined the counters along with an array of plastic cups and bottles of soda.

"Hi, Jayden. What are you doing here?"

Groaning, Jayden banged the heel of her hand against her forehead. "I completely forgot the sleepover tonight. I had to leave early this morning and Luke took the boys to school."

"So I heard already. I think it's great that you're staying with him while they get alarm systems installed in your house and your mom's."

"That was Luke's idea. He said we shouldn't be there without one anymore."

"He's right."

Jayden sat at the kitchen table. "Where are all

these boys that you've insanely agreed to let sleep over at your house?"

Leigh finished arranging the last box of pizza then took a seat next to Jayden. "I threatened them with no food if they came in here before I called them. They're playing tag football in the backyard."

"Good for you. This might be the only few minutes of peace you'll get until tomorrow."

She laughed. "I imagine you're right. The boys tell me that Luke is in his room and you're in a guest room next to them. What kind of sleeping arrangement is that? At least tell me he's sneaking into your room."

"Don't be ridiculous. We don't have that kind of relationship and I'm certainly not going to start one with Elliot and Garrett right there."

"Oh, all right. I can understand that. But tonight you have pure freedom, so make the most of it."

Her friend was right. Tonight she and Luke would be alone in the house. She was excited and scared at the same time.

Across from her, Leigh laughed. "You look as if you're about to open a beautifully wrapped package, but you think it could contain a bomb."

She grinned. "That's exactly how I feel."

"Don't worry so much, Jayden. Everybody feels that way about new relationships. Who knows how it's going to turn out? If you're going to have a relationship, you couldn't do better than Luke."

"So I keep hearing."

"That's because it's true. Don't be so skeptical."

"I guess you're right." She got to her feet. "I'll go say hi to the boys then head home. I'm beat."

"Great. And don't worry about picking Garrett and Elliot up early in the morning. After lunch is fine."

She nodded as she went to the back door. Luke had arranged for the security system and for a service to help clean her house while they stayed with him. It had effectively kept them at his house all week and would likely keep them there a few days after her mother returned. Jayden had to admit she would feel much safer going home knowing the security system was in place. She'd never had anyone to take care of things for her and with the stress she'd had in her life since moving back, having someone to lean on was a relief. She tried to forget that they'd be spending their first night alone together as she stepped into the backyard to check on Garrett and Elliot.

JAYDEN FINISHED HER HAIR and put the hair dryer into the drawer. Luke had called before she'd reached home to say he'd be late because he'd had to drive out of town to meet with a client. It had seemed like a good time to take a long hot shower. When she opened the door to the bathroom between the bedroom she was using and the one the boys used, she noticed the hall light was on as well as the light in Luke's bedroom.

"Luke." She stepped closer to his door and could hear water running from the faucet in his bathroom.

"Luke."

The door opened and Luke appeared with his lower half wrapped in a towel. He wiped his face with a washcloth.

"Hey, I started to knock on the door when I came in but I didn't want to scare you. Where are the dogs?"

"They're in the backyard. I closed the gates so they'd stay inside."

Luke nodded and Jayden didn't attempt further conversation because she was fascinated by the droplets of water glistening on Luke's shoulders. Or maybe it was the way the towel hung low on his hips. His smooth stomach moved rhythmically with each breath he took, and the motion mesmerized her. The sight of the washcloth he'd held dropping to the floor brought her attention back to his face.

His eyes had darkened to a deep navy and his lips were slightly parted. In two strides he crossed the space between them and jerked her to his still-damp skin, her thin T-shirt absorbing the moisture. He cupped his hands on each side of her face, forcing her head backward as he covered her mouth with his. When his body shifted against hers, the heat of desire that had been building for weeks engulfed her, along with a rush of satisfaction, completeness. The thought that she'd finally made it home whisked through her brain as Luke lifted her and carried her to the bed.

LUKE HELD THE PLASTIC bowl toward her and she fished out a piece of freshly cut pineapple. After a night of little sleep, they sat at the kitchen table at six in the morning drinking coffee and finally feeding another hunger.

"This is good. I was starving."

Luke laughed. "Probably because we missed dinner."

"We did, didn't we?"

He kissed her mouth, licking at the remaining pineapple juice. "It was worth it," he whispered.

"I agree." Jayden felt the urge to shove the food aside and drag Luke onto the table, even though she should have already had her fill of him. She was beginning to think she had uncovered an addiction.

He smoothed the wrinkle between her eyebrows with his thumb.

"Stop thinking so hard, Jayden."

"What?"

"You're worrying about what's going to happen, but let's take it one day at a time."

"It's frightening."

He caught her hand and brought it to his lips. "I know, but I think this is worth being a little scared."

She nodded. "I think so, too."

He kissed her and she forgot everything else. Right now, her whole world was here, with Luke.

## CHAPTER SIXTEEN

LUKE FLIPPED THE PANCAKES on the griddle while glancing at Jayden who was pulling sausage from the pan. She caught his eye and smiled. Luke felt the rush all the way to his toes. He turned his attention back to their breakfast. He'd been in love before, but with Alicia he hadn't felt the overwhelming urge to change his whole world. Maybe because their lives had been focused on the same thing— their work to end the Militia. He still wanted that. Only now, he wanted his cover to become his real life. Unfortunately, the two didn't go together, and he couldn't lie to Jayden for much longer about who he was.

"I'm going to check on Garrett," she said. "Elliot, could you take over for me?"

Luke watched her leave the kitchen with Kasey at her heels and head to the barn.

Elliot put Breeze on the floor and replaced Jayden at the stove. He slowly stirred the grits.

"What's going on with you guys?"

Luke poured more batter on the hot surface. "What do you mean?"

"Last night when we watched the movies, you two were sitting all close to each other. And don't think we didn't notice you kissing Aunt J. when you thought we couldn't see."

"Oh, that. Are you mad?"

"Do you like her?"

"Of course I like her. I wouldn't have done that if I didn't."

"Are you two going to get married?"

"I don't know. I mean, we only just met. Most of the time people date for a while, years even, before they decide to get married."

Elliot pushed the spoon around in the grainy mixture then set it aside. "What would happen to me and Garrett if you got married?"

Luke dropped his spatula on the counter and went over to the boy, putting a hand on his thin arm and turning him so they were facing each other.

"You and Garrett will always be with Jayden. She's your family and, if she marries again—no matter who it is—you'll be a part of that family. She wouldn't have it any other way. That much I know. You guys come first with her."

"We don't want her to be sad."

"Neither do I, Elliot."

The boy nodded. "So don't make her sad, okay?"

"I'll try not to."

He patted the boy's shoulder and returned to his cooking. He'd been warned, which made what he felt even more frightening. He wouldn't think twice about going head to head with a member of the

Militia. But the idea of taking on this family, maybe even adding to it, had him quivering in his worn Redwing boots.

"I'm done." He flipped the last pancake onto the plate. Elliot watched him without a word as Jayden and Garrett came bursting in the room. Elliot, the man of their house, had spoken and he wasn't giving his position to just anyone. Luke was beginning to think he might not qualify for the job.

AS LUKE TROTTED THOR across the field and onto the trail, Garrett squealed with laughter. Elliot was behind them and Jayden brought up the rear. He'd had to borrow saddles from a couple of friends so he'd have enough for all four of them to go riding. But it was worth it the minute he saw the three of them, excitedly climbing onto their horses. They'd packed drinks and sandwiches into a soft thermal cooler, which Jayden had tied to her saddle, and he'd attached a long lead line to Garrett's horse to be safe. And though there'd been an argument with him over why he couldn't ride the horse alone yet, the boy had finally given in. It was turning into a perfect Sunday afternoon. The weather had finally cooled into a true fall day and they traversed the few miles to the dead lake with plenty of shouting back and forth to each other.

He tethered the horses as the boys ran to the old flat-bottom boat at the edge of the water.

"Can we take the boat out fishing?" Garrett pulled at Luke's shirt when he joined them.

"Sure you can. Jayden and I brought all the stuff down here yesterday."

He'd had to drag Jayden from the bed Saturday before they went to get the boys. He could see she was as glad as he was they'd done it.

"Why don't you all go in the boat and I'll get the horses settled?" Luke suggested. "We can eat when you get back."

Garrett didn't answer because he was already climbing in the boat. Luke watched as they got settled and finally paddled to the right side of the lake. Among the stumps of dead trees, they began tossing their fishing lines in the water. He grit his teeth as he walked to the horse tied nearest the tree line and loosened the bag with their food in it. "Why are you following us?"

He heard the rumble of a low laugh and glanced at Speck, who was leaning against a tree a few yards into the forest.

"How long have you known I was with you?"

"Since we entered the trees. If Dubois knew what a sloppy job you do following people, he'd have you replaced. Now what do you want?"

"I'm keeping an eye on things. Which is not half of what you're doin'. What do you call this? Keepin' a hand on things?"

"Don't you worry about what I'm doing."

"Oh, I'm not. But Bergeron and Dubois aren't so sure you're goin' to get the information they need."

"There is no information. They don't know what Walsh was doing."

"So you keep saying."

"Because it's true. They trust me. They'd tell me if Walsh had talked to them."

"You keep digging, because I'm not sure my boss, I mean, *our* boss is going to buy that. Don't forget who helps pay your bills. It sure ain't this girl."

Luke listened to Speck's footsteps fade as the man disappeared into the shadows of the trees. He wished he'd brought Kasey along. At least then Speck wouldn't have been able to get so close. He'd remember that from now on.

STARING AT THE CLOUDLESS sky an hour after his confrontation with Speck, Luke forced himself to relax. Jayden slid her hand across the blanket to clasp his. They watched as the boys labored at the edge of the trees to build a frame for a shelter. Luke had promised to help them find a cover to make it waterproof so they could use it for camping.

"Are you okay, Luke? You seem distracted this afternoon."

She moved closer so that their legs brushed.

"I'm thinking about Swayze and Walsh. I wish I knew what happened to those two."

"I believe Eric is alive, maybe hiding until it's safe for him to come back."

"I know you don't want to think he was killed, Jayden, but after this much time without a body, it's hard to imagine he's still alive."

"I know, but I believe it, Luke. And I want to find him."

He chewed on his lip for a moment. "Did he say anything to make you think he would go into hiding? Or did you notice something in his house that made you think that?"

She went still next to him. "What makes you think I've been in that house?"

His mind raced. Bergeron had told him, which proved they were having her watched even when he wasn't around. He never used to make these kinds of slipups. Now he had to try to cover his butt.

"Elliot told me."

It was a lie he could easily get caught in, and obviously, a good one, since she relaxed beside him and smiled. "Elliot talks too much. I did go in the house to see if anything would jump out at me, but nothing did. That doesn't mean he's not still alive."

At the moment, Luke didn't like himself much at all. "You don't mind if I ask the boys about him, do you? They might have heard him talking, maybe on the phone. You know how people think kids aren't listening when they are."

Jayden laughed. "Yeah, I'm learning that myself. You can ask them, but I doubt you'll get much. They don't seem to remember Eric discussing his work."

Luke nodded as Jayden inched even closer to him.

He let his fingers brush across the back of her hand, then her wrist. "Elliot has noticed the change in our relationship."

"What did he say?"

"He wanted to know what would happen to him and Garrett if we got married."

"No way. Does he think I'll ship them off so it can be just the two of us?"

"I think maybe he did."

She sat up so she could see the boys. "I was kidding. Does he truly think that?"

Luke pulled her head down to his chest. "There's been so much change for them lately, I'm sure he expects more anytime."

"He should know I'm not going to abandon them. I already left behind everything to come raise them."

"That's what I told him."

"Well, I'll tell him again this evening."

He kissed the top of her head. "That would make him feel better. I told him he didn't have a thing to worry about."

"I'm sorry he's asking you that kind of stuff. We've barely started seeing each other and he's already worried about us getting married."

"It's okay. Besides, I think we're beyond the point of saying we're only seeing each other. Don't you?"

She was still against him for several seconds before she answered. "You're right. But I don't want you to be pressured to feel something you don't because of Garrett and Elliot. We're both adults here, and we both have physical needs."

Luke's stomach knotted. He wasn't so sure he was following this conversation, but he didn't like the turn it seemed to be taking.

"Are you saying what's happening between us is nothing more than meeting a biological need?"

"I'm saying we like each other and we were alone

in the house together. What happened was natural and I don't want you to think I expect you to marry me next week."

This time Luke jerked to a sitting position. "Damn it, Jayden. I've spent two years not getting close to any woman in this town, especially a parent of one of the kids I coach. And I had numerous offers. I'm not doing this because my baser instincts are out of control."

Jayden pushed herself to face him, her lips in a thin tight line. A swift urge to kiss her nearly overcame him, but he wasn't sure if she would hit him and it would support her point that what had happened between them was nothing more than physical desire.

"You don't have to tell me how lucky I am to be chosen over all the other possible candidates."

"Is that what you think I'm saying? That I chose you out of a lineup?" He rubbed his hand across his forehead. Didn't she feel what he did? Had he been wrong about that?

"Jayden, I'm confused here. I have feelings for you and you're making it sound as if I don't. As if you don't have feelings for me."

She stared at the blanket, tracing a pattern with her finger, until he couldn't stand it anymore. The longer she went without answering him the tighter the band around his chest got. He was beginning to have trouble breathing. He slid his thumb under her chin to bring her head up so she had to look at him.

"Jayden, I'm trying to tell you I love you. I'm not sure how it happened but it has."

She put her hand over his. "I know. I love you, too. I thought when I fell in love again it would be fun and excitement like when I was a teenager. I didn't expect it to be so overwhelming."

He pulled her against his chest, putting his arms around her and feeling hers circle his waist. "It's going to be all right." And while he held her, he almost believed it.

## CHAPTER SEVENTEEN

SHE SMILED AND SAID HELLO without slowing her step for fear she'd be stopped yet again on her way down Main Street. The fall air had turned brisk, which made people want to comment on what a beautiful day it was. But today, Jayden had somewhere to be and didn't have time for pleasantries.

She turned the corner and hurried down a block to the large white house that had been renovated and transformed into the town's public library. The historical society sign that hung on a black iron post read circa 1849. Jayden climbed the sweeping steps to the porch, lined with giant columns supporting a second-floor balcony. She hadn't appreciated the architecture when she was younger and now she simply didn't have time. She made a mental note to bring the boys here one Saturday.

At the front desk, she asked where the computers were, then followed the directions to what might have once been a living room. Jayden stopped short. Amy sat in front of a computer tapping on the keyboard, and beside her, pointing to the screen, was Kent. The two looked up, and Amy smiled, waving her over.

"Hey, Jayden. Kent stopped by. He's helping me get started."

"You told him what you're doing."

Amy paused. "I did. I mean, it's not like he's going to tell anyone in my family."

"Are you sure?"

Kent leaned back in the wooden chair and frowned. "I'm not going to tell anyone. I think it's a great idea."

Jayden eyed him suspiciously. "What are you doing here, anyway?"

This time Amy frowned, but Kent only shook his head. "I was copying articles from old town newspapers. I'll get going now that you're here."

Jayden took Kent's chair when he left and Amy shook her head. "Why were you so mean to him? If anything, he should be the one mad at you."

"What happened to his girlfriend wasn't my fault, but if something happens to you because I suggested you come here and do this, I *will* be responsible. I don't want him to let this slip to the wrong person. And what if you were seen with him and Bergeron heard of it? He might get the idea you were having an affair with Kent. Then holy hell would break loose."

Amy turned back to the screen. "You're right. He was only here for a minute, though, and I don't think many Militia use the library first thing in the morning. I wouldn't have talked to him if I'd thought it would make trouble for either one of us. He's a nice guy."

"Yes, he is. Looks like he's got you set up."

Amy nodded. "Yes. I'm logged into the class now. Thanks so much for suggesting this, Jayden. I don't think I'd have had the nerve to start college courses online on my own. And I'd never have thought to use the library computers. Bergeron won't let me use the one at home. He says it's for his business only."

"What is his business exactly?"

"Don't be that way, Jayden. He's a contractor and they build houses. You know that."

Jayden adjusted her position in the chair. "I'm sorry, Amy. I worry about you and I don't really understand what's between you and Joseph Bergeron."

Amy was quiet for a moment as she read instructions on the computer screen then tapped at a few keys before responding distractedly. "He wanted me and my father told me that was how it was going to be."

Jayden chewed her lip. Things could have been so different for Amy if Mark hadn't been killed. She put her hand on the girl's knee. "I'd help you get away from here if you wanted me to."

"They could find me. My father has contacts all over, and I promise you, if one of his kids doesn't do what he wants, he'll make them fall in line. You should know that."

"I guess I thought he might go easier on you."

"My dad doesn't go easy on anyone."

Jayden rested an elbow on the table. "I'm sorry."

Amy tried to smile. "Me, too." She paused then forced her lips upward. "This makes me feel better, taking this college course and starting to work toward a degree. Maybe one day I might get a job and support myself in case things change. One day I might get the opportunity to start over."

Amy turned back to the computer, and Jayden watched her work. "Looks like you've got the hang of this already, so I'll head back to work. I'll stop by day after tomorrow and check on you. If you need anything in between, call me."

"Okay. How's the puppy?"

"Spoiled rotten and trying to rule all of us. I'll bring him with me next time I come."

"That would be great, thanks."

Jayden hurried from the room, glancing back once. Maybe Mark had felt trapped like this, too. She hoped, for Amy's sake, that things would change very soon. It wasn't fair that Dubois could have so much influence in the woman's life, even if he was her father. But then he'd had a lot of influence in her life, too.

THE GUY FROM THE security company went through the procedure for using the alarm one last time as Jayden checked the step-by-step directions she'd written. She and the boys had made several trips to get their home back in order. Even her mom's system was installed and she could feel safe alone at night.

"Are you scared to stay here tonight, Aunt J.?" Elliot stood beside her on the porch holding the squirming puppy as they watched the security man leave.

"No, not with this alarm. Besides, I'm sure whoever broke in could see we didn't have much to steal and has told all the other criminals not to waste their time."

Elliot laughed and put Breeze on the ground. "That's not true. Robbers don't talk to each other about who doesn't have stuff to steal. I heard Luke say he thought it was the Militia looking for something Mr. Eric might have left here."

"You hear too much."

"Do you think they'll find Mr. Eric soon?"

She rubbed the top of his head. "I hope so."

He ran down the steps to chase the dog who'd found an old tennis ball and was trying to get his mouth around it. She went back into the kitchen and began gathering pasta and sauce to make spaghetti. She found a pan and soon had the meat sizzling.

"Can I be invited for dinner?"

She whirled around to find Luke standing in the doorway.

"Elliot said to come on in."

"You surprised me: I didn't hear you drive up."

He crossed the room to her, his body brushing against hers as she stirred the sauce.

"I'm going to miss you guys at my house. I went by there first and it's so quiet."

She kept staring at the swirling red liquid in front of her. "We're thankful that you let us stay with you."

His hand closed over hers as she held the spoon and he carefully took it from her, placing it on the saucer next to the stove. He turned her around, wrapping her in his arms, and she automatically encircled his waist. He dipped his head to kiss her.

He'd likely intended it to be a quick peck, but the feel of him next to her took her breath and she held him tighter, deepening the kiss. He groaned and pushed her back against the counter.

"Ew, that's gross."

Luke jerked away and Jayden's fingers touched her lips before she smiled.

"You won't always think that, buddy," Luke said with a grin to Garrett who stood in the doorway.

"I'm going outside if you guys are going to keep doing that kissing stuff in here."

"We're all done now and I'm cooking," Jayden said, picking up the spoon.

Garrett shook his head. "I'll go outside anyway just in case."

Luke laughed as the boy disappeared. "They don't seem to be angry about you and me, do they?"

"No, they like you."

"I care about them and you. I want you to know that, and that I meant what I said the other day by the lake."

He stopped and she thought he might be finished even though she felt like he had more he wanted to say. He remained quiet as he scratched at an invisible speck on the counter. When she'd nearly decided he wasn't going to continue, he did.

"There are things in my life right now, Jayden, that keep me from making a big commitment."

The words seemed to burst out of him and she tried not to flinch. She'd only just begun to get used to the idea of loving him and him loving her. Now he seemed to be pulling back. She took a calming breath, reminding herself this whole relationship was new for both of them. "So tell me about them, though I'm not asking for a big commitment."

"I can't." He paused as though he might share more, even moved his lips. But he pressed them together and closed his fist so tightly his knuckles turned white. "I just can't. Not now."

Her heart skipped then beat harder. "Now you're sounding strange."

He shook his head. "Don't worry. We'll talk more, later. Let's try and keep things the way they are for now."

She stirred the sauce again and reminded herself that Luke had taken care of them and she didn't need to be afraid that he was hiding something. He was more likely a little nervous about taking on a woman with a ready-made family.

"We don't have to make any big commitments right now."

He nodded.

He'd obviously decided to quit talking and she figured changing the subject would make them both more comfortable. "Why don't you get that French bread out of the freezer? Helping in the kitchen will score you bonus points with me."

"You're easy."

"That's not nice."

He laughed. "You know what I meant."

"To be honest with you, I have been kind of a pushover."

He put the bread on the counter. "You weren't in

the beginning, but once you got to know me, my charm seemed to overwhelm you."

She waved the spoon at him, splattering sauce on the stove. "Overwhelm, huh?"

He grinned. "Well, with a little work on my part."

"You get your part of this meal done and then I'll be overwhelmed."

He opened the bread and flipped through her cabinets until he found a flat pan to put it on. He stuck the pan in the warm oven.

"There, I'm done. You're overwhelmed. Like I said, easy."

The commotion of yelling kids and barking dogs rang through the house as Elliot and Garrett came in from outside.

"Since I'm so easy maybe you should take on that bunch."

"Nothing wrong with being easy," he muttered as he started toward the living room.

WHEN LUKE PUSHED OPEN the door to his house, he knew they were waiting for him. Joseph Bergeron sat forward in the recliner, his elbows on his knees.

"Ah, Luke, home at last and finally alone again. So did you get the information we need while you had the family here?"

"They don't know anything. I've questioned all three of them repeatedly, but they don't have a clue what Walsh knew."

"Or are you so involved that you might not tell me if they did know?"

"I know what my job is."

"I never expected you to enjoy it this much. But that's not why I'm here. Let's go out by the pool."

As they stepped into the crisp night air, Luke saw a figure sitting at his patio table. He glanced at Bergeron. "What's this?"

"An opportunity for you. Don't screw it up."

He followed Bergeron to the table and immediately recognized Paul Dubois.

"Luke, good to see you again," Dubois said. Luke took the empty chair across from him.

"We want you involved in a very big project we're working on."

"Which is?"

Dubois laughed. "It's going to be important to a lot of people. We've got a month to finish preparations. What we need from you is an honest opinion on whether or not the Miller girl or her kids have any idea what that reporter was on to."

Luke didn't expect to get a full answer from the man. They'd never tell him more than what they felt was absolutely necessary. "No, they don't have information. If they did I'd have found out by now."

"What about the location of the reporter? Do they know where he is?" Dubois asked.

Luke tried not to tighten his hands on the chair. "I assume he's dead, and I guess they do, too. Or is there something I'm not aware of? Swayze killed him, right?"

"As far as we know, Swayze didn't kill Walsh. He was working with him. We think Swayze killed someone and buried the body parts with Walsh's watch to lead people astray. I'm sure he knew the police would eventually find that Walsh wasn't the one buried, but it would give him extra time. Of course, Swayze lived in his own world anyway."

The words took Luke by surprise. "That doesn't make sense. Why would Swayze work with a reporter to expose the Militia? He was in the Militia."

"We don't know for sure," Dubois said. "We started watching Swayze when Walsh began visiting him. We think Duke had gotten into his mind that we were his enemy. He was paranoid about people being after him. That's how we figured out they were working together, and that Swayze was feeding information to the reporter. If Walsh is dead, we didn't do it. We think he's hiding. Don't know where, though."

Luke remembered the spot in the barn outside Swayze's house. They'd thought the reporter had hidden there to watch Duke's house. Instead it had been the Militia watching the two of them. But where was Walsh now?

Dubois slid his chair back. "You keep trying to find out about our missing reporter and while you're at it pay another visit to our friend you met with in Boyden."

"William Lebeaux?"

"That's right. Our friend Will is withholding information. He's concerned about his safety once he's shared what we sent him to get. He might even have talked to the FBI. Be sure to tell him that if he causes enough trouble we'll kill him, information be damned."

Luke nodded as the other men stood and Dubois walked away.

"We'll be in touch," Bergeron said as he started after Dubois.

"Did you find what you were looking for at her house?" Luke asked.

Bergeron paused and turned back. "Do you mean the Miller girl's house?"

"Of course that's who I mean."

"Luke, if we'd found what we were looking for you'd know. Then you wouldn't have to fool with her anymore. But maybe you're not minding that so much, I'm thinking." Bergeron eyed him for a second more then disappeared into the darkness.

Still sitting, Luke rubbed his fingers on the table. William Lebeaux had mentioned Dubois was planning an operation that would take place in a month. Those plans had something to do with the military base in Boyden, but he couldn't imagine why the Loyalists would be interested in a base that had been on the chopping block for a year now. What was so important about a place the government didn't even want to keep open?

## CHAPTER EIGHTEEN

THE MINIATURE BALL of fur squirmed in Amy's lap. Jayden sat beside her at the library's computer, the purse-sized doggie tote on the floor next to her. She'd slipped the dog in to visit with Amy, just as she'd promised. She doubted the librarian would care, but it was often better to ask forgiveness than to ask permission.

"Jayden, I've got the hang of it now, so you don't have to keep leaving work to come help me on your lunch break."

"It's okay. We were slow."

"Thanks for bringing Breeze with you. He looks happy."

"The boys love him and Kasey's completely adopted him. But he's still yours, so you can get him back when you're ready."

The younger woman shook her head. "Joseph would never allow me to have a small dog like this again. He hated it."

"Maybe you won't have to worry about what he wants one day."

"Maybe."

"He doesn't know you're coming here for this online algebra class, does he?"

Amy thumbed through her notebook. "No. He thinks I volunteer at the library. He knows I like to read and I bring books home."

"Good. I'd hate for him to stop you from getting an education."

Amy handed the dog to Jayden and picked up her pencil. "He's not going to find out."

Jayden bent to put the dog in the carrier but Amy stopped her. "Wait, I need to talk to you. I keep avoiding it because you'll get mad at me."

She straightened, holding the dog next to her stomach. "Don't be silly, Amy. I'm not going to get mad at you."

Amy doodled in her notebook before speaking. "You're dating that lawyer, Luke Taylor, aren't you?"

"Sort of. I mean, I guess we're dating. It's one of those things that happened unexpectedly. He's my nephew's baseball coach and we were around each other a lot." She stopped abruptly when she realized she was babbling.

"Be careful, Jayden."

The warning took her by surprise. "What do you mean?"

"I think he's somehow mixed up with the Loyalists."

Jayden's muscles constricted until she thought she might not be able to get a breath. "Have you seen him with them?" she finally forced out. "Are you saying he meets with Joseph Bergeron?"

"No. I haven't seen them meet. But he's represented a lot of them."

"He's the public defender. He has to represent people who can't afford their own attorneys."

"Do you think the Militia can't afford to pay an attorney?"

Jayden paused. She was defending Luke against Amy's accusations even though they were the same ones she'd made in the beginning. "Are you certain he's working with Bergeron and your dad?"

"No, but I'm pretty sure. I've heard his name mentioned frequently, even if I've never seen them talk. But then they wouldn't do that in public. All I'm saying is keep your eyes open."

Jayden nodded and shifted the dog into the carrier. "I will. And I'm not mad, Amy. Don't ever be afraid to talk to me. I can handle anything."

The woman nodded. "I didn't want you to feel as if you were repeating history because of how everything went with my brother."

Hearing footsteps on the wooden floor, Jayden whispered goodbye and hurried from the room. Amy was right. She did feel as if she was repeating the past. She'd be more careful this time. She wouldn't let others get hurt, although she knew she was beyond the point of protecting herself. If what Amy said about Luke was true, it would break her heart.

THE WIND WHIPPED Luke's freshly cut hair as he made his way through the trees. Evette Miller was the kind of barber he needed. One who heard every piece of news or gossip at least two days before the general public. She never minded sharing her bulletins with him. "I know this won't go any farther if I tell you," she'd always say. He never repeated the things she told him to the Cypress Landing residents, but if it was important he did pass her information on to others.

Through the cracks in the old barn a shadowy image moved. Charles Greer was there, waiting for him. Luke hurried inside.

"Well, Taylor, I was beginning to think we might have to pull you in. I hadn't heard from you in so long I wondered if maybe you'd gone to the other side."

"Don't be ridiculous."

Greer shrugged. "It does happen."

Luke gritted his teeth. "Not with me."

The older man stuck his hands in his pockets. "I hope you've got something because we haven't been able to find any information about what's going on down here."

"Dubois and his crew are making big plans. I think the Loyalists are definitely working with the bigger group, and whatever they're up to is going to happen within the next month. It involves that military base near Boyden. The one they're going to close."

Charles's face wrinkled and in the dim light Luke could see his eyes focusing on the other side of the building as the man ran through different scenarios in his mind. Luke had already done the same thing and come up with nothing. Until he'd had a haircut today and heard an interesting tidbit of information.

"Evette Miller, who cuts my hair, also dates the retired general, Arneaux."

Greer nodded.

"She said he'd invited her to attend a reception at this particular military base for a group of visiting senators, next month. These senators are pushing for the closure of this base."

"You don't think they'd try something while the senators are there?" The older agent looked doubtful.

"That sounds exactly like what they'd do. What better way to tell the committee they're against base closings? I believe the reporter stumbled onto this plot and when they tried to kill him he went into hiding."

"So you think Walsh could still be alive?"

Luke shrugged. "It's what the Militia believes. Dubois said so last night."

"But wouldn't he come home for his stuff or find a contact, maybe that girl who owned the house he rented?"

"No, she doesn't know anything and he hasn't contacted her."

"How can you be sure he hasn't?"

"She'd have told me."

Greer arched an eyebrow. "Would she? What is it you're not saying?"

Luke didn't answer. He'd known the older man too long to lie to him.

"Luke, this woman used to be a Loyalist."

"That's not really true. She wasn't involved."

"What if you're wrong? Maybe she's figured out

you're FBI and she's going to turn you over to Dubois for a price?"

"Now you're talking crazy. She wouldn't do that."

Charles shook his head. "So you've got it bad, huh?"

Luke stared at the floor, then nodded.

"I hope you're not making a mistake here, Taylor. If she wasn't in it before, she is now simply by associating with you."

Luke jerked his head up. "Don't you think I know that? The Militia is convinced Walsh gave her information he'd found on them and I'm not sure how far they're willing to go to see if it's true."

"What will you do?"

"Keep up my role with the Militia. But I'm going to protect Jayden and her family while I'm at it."

"That's a nice thought. I hope you realize that those two things might cross paths in a really bad way before this is over. You may have to choose one or the other."

Luke scuffed the ground with his boot. "I know." He wasn't sure if Charles heard him. His throat had tightened on the words. He looked at the older man. "I've spent my life bringing the Militia to justice."

"I'm saying you may have to choose between that and this woman. You could easily compromise your cover by protecting her. You've worked too hard and lost a lot to get this close to the Militia. Now you're going to let it all go because you're in love? Where's the Luke Taylor who doesn't let anything get in his way?"

Raking his fingers through his hair, Luke tried to

stop the tightness in his throat from spreading to his chest. "Let's hope it doesn't come to that."

Charles was quiet for a moment. "All right then. We'll start gathering information about the senators' next trip, and you keep us filled in on what's going on over here. I wish our team could have found more to help you, but we'll keep looking." Luke nodded. Charles started toward the door, but paused and looked back. "Try not to get too attached to this woman, Taylor. It's only going to make trouble later on."

Luke didn't have a response, but it didn't matter because Charles Greer disappeared into the night. Luke was beyond just being attached to Jayden. He loved her and her family—mother, dogs, kids, all of them. He couldn't reveal who he was and stay with her in Cypress Landing because Paul Dubois would kill him. She had moved all the way from California to raise the boys in what was home to them, so he couldn't ask her to start again elsewhere. He had to get the Militia leaders behind bars so he could have a chance at a normal life.

JAYDEN STUCK HER HEAD into Elliot's bedroom. "Dinner will be ready in five minutes. What in the world is all this mess?"

Only Elliot's shoes were visible, sticking out of the closet door. Around his feet, he'd piled what had to be half the contents of his closet. Slowly he backed his way out.

"I'm looking for one of my old school notebooks. I had written stories and stuff in it and my teacher said to bring them. We're making a book of our writing and she said I could use things I'd already done."

"And you think it's in there."

"I know it is." He crawled back into the closet and returned waving a blue notebook. "See, this is it."

"Wonders never cease. You should take that pile as a hint that maybe you need to do a little house-cleaning."

Elliot began shoving the mountain of junk back. "I'll do it another day."

"Elliot."

"Okay, okay. I'll do it after we eat."

"Good."

Back in the kitchen, Jayden set the table and gave one last shout for the boys.

After filling their plates, they dropped into chairs at the table. Elliot propped the notebook beside his glass.

"At the table, Elliot?"

"I used to keep it with me all the time and jot down funny things that happened. I want to use them to make the stories for the book we're putting together in class. I thought I'd bring it with me since it still has a few empty pages."

"You're expecting us to have an event worth writing down while we eat."

He grinned. "You never know."

From the back of the house they heard a bark and the clickety-click of dog toenails on the wood floor. Breeze appeared with a stuffed animal in his mouth.

Kasey raced after him with his head low, determined to capture the toy. The pup headed straight for the table and leapt into Garrett's lap. Kasey followed and planted both feet on Garrett's leg and proceeded to wrestle the toy from the smaller dog. The glass of milk that had been in Garrett's hand went flying through the air and Jayden said a quick prayer of thanks for plastic cups.

"Kasey, stop it!" She took hold of the dog's collar and pushed him out the kitchen door. The puppy still sat on Garrett's lap, the stuffed rat hanging by its tail from his mouth.

"And you, you little instigator, are going to the bedroom."

She carried Breeze to Garrett's room and shut the door.

When she got back the two boys were laughing as they wiped up the spilled milk, then Elliot sat down with his pen. "See, I told you, things happen."

"At least finish eating before you start writing."

"I'm only going to make a note so I won't forget anything."

She wondered what the teacher would think if he kept track of all the interesting moments around here. She'd probably wonder how they survived.

WITH THE LAST PLATE in the dishwasher, Jayden shut the door and turned on the machine. She wondered where Luke was tonight. She hadn't heard from him all day and, after Amy's revelation, she wasn't sure what she'd say to him. Maybe she wouldn't say anything. Amy could be wrong. Jayden didn't see how the man she knew could be Militia.

"Aunt J."

She looked up from the dishwasher to Elliot, who came into the kitchen holding his notebook.

"Did you get your closet cleaned?"

"Yes, ma'am."

"Good. I'd hate to think I had done the kitchen cleanup by myself for nothing."

The boy shifted his weight from one foot to the other.

"You okay?"

Climbing onto a bar stool at the small island, he placed the bound pages in front of him. "I found something weird in here."

"What kind of weird?"

He sifted through the book to a page near the back. "Mr. Eric wrote in here, but I'd never seen it before now."

Jayden crossed the kitchen to him. "When would he have done that?"

"I wrote in this a lot last spring when he was around, but I put it away at the end of the school year. He did go in my closet to get a bat for us one evening, remember?"

She leaned over him to look at the writing, scribbled in pencil.

*I'm putting a note here in hopes that if anything happens to me one of you will find it. I know Elliot has this thing with him most of the time. I've found a man in the Militia who's willing to help me. Most*

*people don't have much respect for him and they
think he's crazy but it's all really an act. Or at least I
hope so...*

There were a couple of skipped lines, then more.

*The Loyalists are cooking up a scheme to try and
stop the closing of a military base near here. They're
planning to bomb the area when the senate committee comes to visit. Several men arrived at the camp
last week from another Militia group. They weren't
some ragtag bunch, real military people. They're
watching me now, I don't know how much. My contact
says the safe house is ready. He took my watch and
said he'd plant it on a body that was buried on his
property last night. We'll be leaving in a few hours.*

"Will this help find Eric?"

"I don't know yet, Elliot."

"What will you do with this, Aunt J.?"

"We have to tell the investigator. And you'll need
to let me hang on to it." She picked up the book and
Elliot nodded, jumping to the floor. "I'm going to
play with Kasey."

"Okay." She stared at the page for a minute.
"Elliot." He turned back to her. "Don't say a word to
anyone about this right now, okay? It will be our
secret, except I'm going to call Mr. Cooper."

"All right. But aren't you going to tell Luke?"

"Maybe later. For now we should keep it between
us and the sheriff's office. I'm sure that's how they
will want it."

"I guess so." He flipped on the outside light and
went out to the backyard, Kasey trailing him.

Jayden reached for the phone on the counter and held it in her hand, staring at the keypad. She'd have to get the phone book to find Jackson Cooper's home number. She'd made a conscious decision to keep this from Luke after what Amy had told her today. How could she love a man she couldn't trust? She shook her head. It wasn't that she didn't trust him, but it was the way the police would want things, just like she'd told Elliot.

She found the phone book in the drawer and flipped through the pages, then slowly punched the number.

JAYDEN EYED JACKSON, who ran his finger over the words on the page. "No idea where or what this safe house is?" he asked.

She shook her head. "I can't think of any place Eric would think was safe."

"Maybe Swayze had the safe house."

Jayden shrugged. "I've been gone for ten years. You're more likely to know that than I am."

"I'll have to check into it." He closed the book. "Who all knows about this?"

"Only Elliot, who found it, and me."

"You haven't told Taylor?"

"No."

Jackson tapped the counter for a moment. "Don't."

The word hung in the air and from the backyard she could hear Kasey barking and Elliot laughing. She wanted to escort the investigator out and shut the door. She didn't want to know what was behind

Jackson's statement, but for the safety of her family she had to hear.

"Are you going to explain that?"

He studied the notebook in his hand briefly. "I know there's a relationship between you two. I don't pay much attention to gossip, but I do hear it. I don't trust Taylor. I see him with too many of the Militia's flunkies to believe he hasn't been on their payroll. He doesn't need to know what you've found."

She nodded. He was right. First Amy and now Jackson were telling her the same thing. Don't trust the man. Hadn't she been in this situation before? Last time people had been killed. If Luke worked with the Militia, she couldn't trust him, couldn't love him. Even though she already did. She simply had to make herself stop.

## CHAPTER NINETEEN

AN IMPROMPTU MEETING on such short notice wasn't usually a good sign and, as Luke stared across the table at Bergeron, he was afraid things were about to get much worse than he'd imagined a lot sooner than he'd hoped.

"So what's in this notebook the sheriff supposedly has, Joseph?"

Bergeron scratched at a spot on the table. "They definitely have a book. But they're keeping it quiet. Not even my guy at the sheriff's office has more information than the fact that the book exists and it's about Walsh. But he says it looks like a kid's notebook. I'm thinking there are only two kids who might have access to what Walsh wrote down. Now, what do you know about it?"

"I tell you I don't know anything. I don't believe it came from her kids. Jayden hasn't mentioned a notebook to me and I talked to her this morning."

"Well, the notebook appeared at the sheriff's office last night with Jackson Cooper. Maybe our girl has made you."

"What is that supposed to mean?"

"That she knows you're working with us and she isn't going to tell you anything."

Luke pushed away from the table and paced across the room.

"That's crazy. She has no reason to suspect me."

"Something is going on and you're not getting what we need so we may have to take matters into our own hands."

Luke planted his feet on the wooden floor. "Let me handle it. If they've got information I'll get it."

"You do that, and then we'll see."

Luke missed the bottom step as he left the building, his foot landing with a jolt on the ground. He scrambled through the trees back to his boat. He had to see Jayden, now. He couldn't tell her everything, but maybe he could get enough out of her to pacify the Militia. What he couldn't understand was why Jayden hadn't told him if she'd found notes from Walsh. Didn't she trust him? He laughed bitterly to himself. If she hadn't trusted him before, after tonight she definitely wouldn't.

HE COULD TELL SOMETHING was different when he walked into the room. The kitchen had always felt warm and welcoming, but now a slight chill made him shiver.

Jayden was at the stove cooking.

"Where are the boys?"

"They went to the Fontenots' to camp out in their backyard, since they don't have school in the morning."

He crossed to where she stood and wrapped his arms around her. She stiffened at first then relaxed.

"What are you making this late? It's after nine o'clock."

"Crawfish soup. All the boys are coming to Mom's for lunch tomorrow."

He peered into the pot. "Crawfish soup, that sounds interesting."

She snorted and stirred in the liquid. "It's not fancy, but it's good. By the way, I tried to get in touch with Kent today to ask about an old friend from high school but I couldn't catch up to him. Have you seen him?"

"No, he didn't come to work today and I couldn't get him at home or on his cell, which is unusual for Kent. He's never missed work without letting me know." Luke noticed that she abruptly stopped stirring.

"Do you think he's all right? What if he's home sick and can't get out of bed?"

"I had his landlord check his house. He's not there. I imagine he ran to visit his mom and forgot to tell me. I'm going to give her a call in the morning."

She didn't respond, but seemed to relax.

He flicked a crumb across the counter and watched her, unsure how to start.

"The sheriff's office brought in evidence that might be a lead to Walsh's whereabouts."

The muscles in her hand twitched as they tightened on the spoon. Bergeron had been right. She knew.

"How did you find out, Luke?"

He shrugged. "I've been keeping up with the investigation."

She glanced at him then picked up a bottle of seasoning and shook it into the soup. "Why?"

"My client ended up dead because he allegedly killed someone whose body we can't find."

She nodded but didn't speak. It was time to get to the point. "Did you give them the notebook?" he asked.

She whacked the spoon hard on the side of the pot and banged it onto a saucer. "What makes you think they got it from me?"

With her facing him like this the lies became harder and harder to tell. "I heard that the sheriff's office had a kid's notebook with references to Walsh. I wondered if it might belong to one of the boys."

"Really? Well, I would think if you got that much information you'd have found out where the notebook came from."

"I wasn't told that."

"And who exactly filled you in on all this?"

She was angrier than he'd expected and he began to sense that maybe he wasn't the only one with secrets brewing under the surface. "It's not important. Why didn't you tell me?"

"It was Elliot's book. Now, who gave you this information?"

He lowered his head in defeat. How deep was she in this mess? Had she known more all along? He wasn't sure exactly what he could tell her that she would believe. "I spoke with Detective Cooper."

Jayden caught the edge of the counter because she didn't know what else to do with her hands, other than perhaps smack the man standing next to her. Lies. The room had become so full of lies they seemed to suck the air out, leaving her gasping.

"Get out."

His eyes widened. "What's wrong, Jayden?"

"You're lying to me, Luke, and I'll bet this isn't the first time, either. I don't even want to know all the lies. Jackson Cooper would never have told you about that notebook because he asked me not to tell you. He doesn't trust you. He believes you're working with the Militia. And I think he might be right."

"It's not like that, Jayden. I promise."

He took a step toward her and she jerked a knife out of the block on the counter. Pointed it at him. "I said get out."

Luke's fists knotted at his side and he banged them against his leg. "You and the boys could be in danger."

"So I see. I don't think I can trust you to be the one to protect us."

He didn't speak immediately, but wiped his hand over his face from forehead to chin. His skin seemed pale. "You're wrong. I can protect you. You've got to let me explain."

"I don't need an explanation from you. Now leave and don't come back here. You won't be welcome."

He paced from one wall to the other, but didn't try to come toward her. At the farthest wall he stopped, his back to her. Suddenly, he banged his fist against the window frame. Spinning around he opened his mouth then closed it. After a few seconds, he tried again.

"Jayden, please, I'm undercover FBI. I've been infiltrating the Militia for years."

Her laugh sounded hollow and dead even to her. Was there no end to how far he would go?

"You don't believe me, I know."

"Of course I don't believe you, Luke. What idiot would? Do you think I'm going to jump at any story so I can believe the man I've fallen in love with isn't one of the Militia's servants?"

"I don't belong to the Loyalists."

"I told you to leave." She advanced a step and he stared at her as though he might wrestle her for the knife. Instead, he rubbed his forehead and strode to the kitchen door.

"Watch your back, Jayden."

"What do you think I'm doing?" Her voice cracked, but she held the knife in his direction to be sure he didn't think she might give in to him.

He paused, holding on to the doorknob. "I'm afraid you're going to have a lot more to worry about than me. I'll do everything I can to help you."

Her hand wavered. She wanted to believe that he had her best interest at heart. That he would try to keep them safe, but she couldn't trust him, not now.

The door clicked shut behind him and she sank to the floor, the knife wobbling in her grasp. With her free hand she wiped at the first tear that trickled down her cheek. As more followed she gave up and let them run down her chin. How would she protect herself and the boys without help? And there was an informant within the sheriff's department. They couldn't watch them every minute anyway. The answer lay with Eric Walsh. If they'd found one clue, maybe there were more. Struggling to her feet, she went to Elliot's room and flung open the recently cleaned closet. Placing the knife on the dresser nearby, she began dragging toys, clothes and sports equipment into the middle of the floor. She had to find more and soon.

ONE DAY. IT HAD ONLY BEEN one full day since he'd walked out of Jayden's house and already it felt like an eternity. Luke had met with Charles Greer that night and had more FBI surveillance brought in, but without notifying anyone in the sheriff's office or the city police department. He knew for a fact there was a leak in the sheriff's office, and the city police probably weren't any better. Luke trusted Matt Wright and Jackson Cooper. He couldn't be sure how many eyes would be watching if he or anyone else tried to meet with one of them.

A sudden banging on his office door made him drop the pen he'd been twirling. "Come in."

Kent burst into the room, his usually starched shirt wrinkled and his unruly hair curling around his ears.

"It's about time you showed up, Kent. After two days and not one word from you I was getting ready to file a missing-persons report."

The young man ignored him and walked across the wooden floor to the window. Glancing out, he snapped the blinds shut, then crossed to the front of Luke's desk.

"What's the matter with you, Kent?"

"We need to talk."

"That's obvious. Why don't you sit down?"

Kent slammed his palms onto the desk and Luke's coffee cup vibrated to one side.

"I don't want to sit down. I want you to come clean with me right now."

Luke's heart skipped. Confrontations didn't usually bother him, but he had a good idea what was coming and he didn't want to lie anymore.

"What do you want me to tell you?"

"I want to know about your ties with the Militia."

"What ties? You're being ridiculous, Kent." Luke closed the folder he'd been reviewing.

"I've been told from a reliable source that you work for the Militia. Is it true, Luke?"

Luke pinched the bridge of his nose. His alias was coming apart at the seams. When he looked up, Kent was still staring at him. They had a lot in common. They'd each dragged themselves away from a father determined to see them join the Militia. Except Kent had stayed free of it. Luke had returned to his roots.

He pushed back from his desk. "Let's take a walk."

As they stepped onto the sidewalk, the fall sun blazed down on his head and Luke started toward the park.

"Are you going to talk to me?"

He glanced at the younger man and nodded. When they reached the park he sat at a concrete picnic table and tossed down the legal pad and pen he'd brought with him.

Kent eased onto the bench across from him.

"I try to watch what I say in my office. You never know who might be listening."

"You think the FBI might be interested in your involvement with the Militia?"

Fingering a small twig on the table, Luke chewed the inside of his lip. Years of undercover work were coming to an end. He wasn't sure how he felt about that. With a quick move he snapped the twig. He watched a squirrel scamper across the grass and up a tree. "I guess they are interested, although I'm more worried that the Militia might be listening. I am the FBI, Kent."

"Yeah, right. You're FBI but you get all the Militia off and do their dirty work for them."

"That's my cover. I'm working toward a goal here and I'm very close. Or at least I was."

"Why are you telling me this, Mr. Undercover Man?"

Luke shook his head. "I'm not sure I can maintain my cover and protect the people I care about."

"You're talking about Jayden, aren't you?"

"I am. I guess she told you that she believes I'm working with the Militia."

"No, she didn't."

Luke tilted his head. "Then what made you suspect and come to me like this?"

"It's kind of a long story."

"I've got time."

Kent folded his arms on top of the table. "A few weeks ago, Jayden started helping Bergeron's live-in girlfriend take online college courses."

"She did what!"

"She was trying to help Amy see that she could get away from the Militia, from that life. Her dad gave her to Bergeron like you'd give away a dog, but she didn't know how to leave without them finding her and she only had her high school diploma. She wanted a plan to make a life for herself."

"I'm guessing you got drawn into this."

Kent tugged at a hair that blew across his forehead. "I knew Amy from school. We both grew up in the Militia. I was in the library one day while she was waiting on Jayden. I helped her, and from then on I stopped by when she would go online for her class and I— We got…involved, even though it's only been a short time."

"That can happen."

"The other night Bergeron discovered she was taking classes. I'm not sure how. I imagine he had Amy followed. She came to my place, needed to get away. I said I'd call you, but she wouldn't let me. Told me you were Militia. That she'd heard Bergeron plan meetings with you."

"So what did you do with her?"

"Don't worry about it. I took care of it."

"You still don't trust me. I told you I'm FBI."

"And I can tell you I'm CIA, but that doesn't mean I am."

Luke jerked the legal pad closer and scribbled on it. Then ripped the paper off and shoved it across the table. "Call this number and ask for Charles Greer. Tell him I said it was okay to talk to you."

"What if he asks about you? What do I tell him?"

"That I'll try to finish my job here, but I won't sacrifice Jayden and the boys for it."

Kent leaned back, his eyes wide. "Do you think it's going to come to that?"

"I'm afraid it might."

The younger man watched him a moment longer then folded the paper and stuck it in his shirt pocket. "How can I help?"

"Help what?"

"Protect Jayden."

"No, you stay out of it."

Kent stood, then looked down at him. "When you realize you can't do this all by yourself, let me know what I need to do."

"Let's hope that time never comes."

Kent nodded and walked away. Luke settled the legal pad in front of him and started listing ways he could get the information in the notebook, then get it to the Militia. If he did, maybe they'd decide that was all Eric Walsh had left behind.

WHERE WAS AMY? Jayden opened the back door of the clinic and welcomed the sound of the barking dogs. Maybe they would take her mind off the fact that Amy hadn't been at the library for two days now. She'd dropped the bombshell about Luke, then never showed up again. Yesterday evening Jayden had resorted to calling Kent about her. But no one knew where he was, either. The secretary at Luke's office told her Kent still wasn't at work today. Maybe something had developed between the two, but the least Amy and Kent could have done was let her know were leaving town. She prayed that's all it was and that nothing had happened to them. That Bergeron hadn't caught them together. That idea chilled her to the bone.

She walked into the surgery where she had two animals scheduled for minor surgeries. She'd try Kent again tonight at home. Surely they hadn't done anything stupid—like run away together. Although, personally she longed for Luke to take her away from all this. To say that the Militia connection wasn't true, that they could be happy and love each other. Life didn't work like that, though. She had the boys to consider and her mother. Above all, this was her home. She was back now and wanted to stay here. The Militia had sent her running before, but she'd be damned if she'd run again.

She finally left the clinic as the sky started to darken. The days were getting shorter and the time would change soon, then it would be dark when she came home late. Thank goodness her mom could pick Garrett and Elliot up at school and keep them until she was off.

Pulling into her mother's drive, she was surprised to see the house dark. But the lights were still on in the salon. There weren't any customers' cars in front so her mom must have convinced the boys to let her cut their hair or possibly even help her clean the place. Now that would be a feat.

Halfway to the steps of the building, she paused.

"Hey, what are you guys doing in there? It sure is quiet."

She glanced around trying to see beyond the shadows. Leave it to the three of them to jump out and scare her half to death.

She climbed the steps. "All right, no more hide-and-seek. I don't feel like having a heart attack right now."

Jayden pushed the door open and screamed. Scrambling to her mother's unmoving body, she pressed her fingers against Evette's neck searching for a pulse. Tears of relief ran down her face when she felt it. Her mother moaned and opened her eyes, then closed them.

"Be still, Mom, I'm calling an ambulance. Where are the boys? Did they go to our house?"

Her mother's lips moved and she bent closer to hear.

"They took the boys."

"Who took them?" The words made her sick.

Evette's head moved slightly from side to side. "Don't know who."

Jayden jerked the phone from its cradle and dialed 911. As she automatically made the request for an ambulance, she saw the piece of paper on the counter amid the hairbrushes and the scissors. When she hung up she snatched the paper and sank to her knees.

"They're on their way, Mom. It's going to be fine."

Staring at the note, panic nearly blinded her. The Militia had her boys and they wanted information about Eric. That was going to be a problem, because she didn't know anything and she doubted they'd believe her.

# CHAPTER TWENTY

"I'm sorry, Jayden. It's my fault."

"Mom, it is not your fault. The Militia did this."

"But if we'd been inside with the alarm on and the doors locked—"

"They'd have come in and taken them anyway. No locked door or alarm system would have stopped them."

The older woman wadded the tissue in her hand. "What will you do?"

"I'm going to get the boys back."

"By yourself? Why won't you let Matt and Jackson help you?"

Jayden strode to the window of the small room and studied the hospital parking lot. "The note said no police and that's why I didn't tell them the boys were missing. Remember, they've gone to spend a few days with relatives in Texas. I expect you to go along with that story until I can take care of things."

"We don't have relatives in Texas."

"We do now."

Her mother pushed herself up in the bed, wincing. Then she touched the edges of a cut on her forehead, which had been neatly sealed with a glue-like substance in the emergency room. "What are you planning, Jayden?"

"I can't risk hurting the boys by getting the law involved. They can't know there's a note. The Militia has people in the sheriff's office. If I worked with them, the Militia would hear."

"You can't do this by yourself."

"I don't intend to."

"But who will help you?"

She adjusted her mother's pillow then gave her a wry smile. "The one person I know I can't trust."

IT WAS AFTER ONE in the morning when the hospital doors swished shut behind her. Her mother had finally dozed off, but the staff woke her on a regular basis to assess her head injury.

Sliding behind the wheel of the Tahoe, she spotted a dog chew she'd left in the seat when she dropped the two dogs off at the clinic after closing hours. The animals would be safe in the kennels until this was over. She could use her mom's injury and the fact that she was busy as an excuse to let them stay there where they could have inside shelter and a fenced yard. She was exhausted, but there'd be no sleep for her yet.

Fifteen minutes later, she banged hard on the door until her hand ached. She didn't hear a sound, so she banged again.

"Get up, Luke."

His vehicle was here, but what if he'd taken off, too, like Kent and Amy?

Deep in the house a light glowed and she continued hammering the door with her fist.

"Okay, okay, I'm coming."

The door opened and Luke's eyes widened. He obviously wasn't expecting her. He wore a pair of gym shorts and nothing else and as his hand brushed across his bare chest she wished a thousand things were different.

"I want my boys back."

"What are you talking about?"

"Don't pretend you don't know where they are. You're in up to your eyeballs with the Militia and you're going to help me get my boys back right now."

Luke pressed his fingers to his lips and shook his head. He went inside and she followed him. Disappearing down the hall to his bedroom, he returned immediately with a long-sleeve T-shirt and a pair of tennis shoes. He managed to put them on without stopping his forward progress. Capturing her arm as he passed, he dragged her through the back door and across the yard. At the edge of the barn he finally stopped. His face was shadowed but she swore the concern and worry she saw had to be genuine. Unless Luke was a fantastic actor, which, of course, he might be.

"Are you telling me the Militia took the boys?"

"As if you don't know."

"I promise, Jayden, I didn't know."

"I've got the note they left me. It said no police, but if you ever cared about me, about the boys, you'll help me get them back."

"Of course I'm going to help you."

She paused, trying desperately to read him in the darkness.

"Just like that, you agree?"

"What did you expect?"

"That I'd have to convince you, that you wouldn't turn against your Loyalist buddies that easily."

"They're not my buddies. They're my job, and if you'd given me a chance the other night before you took a butcher knife to me I'd have explained."

"What's to explain?"

"Jayden, I really am FBI. Working with the Militia is what I was sent here to do. It's all I've ever known."

"Oh, please, not that again."

He stalked the ground in front of her. "Would you listen, even if you don't believe me?"

"Fine, tell me your story."

He stopped in front of her and raked his hand through his hair. "I grew up in that life, with my father being the head of a Militia group, kind of like Dubois. When my mom tried to get us out he killed her. Eventually, I ran away and was able to work my way through college, but I devoted my life to destroying the Militia."

"Can you prove this undercover story?"

"What do you want? I could call my boss in and let you meet with him. It might take a few hours."

"Why can't we go to the nearest FBI office and let them identify you?"

"I'm undercover. No one in any office knows who I am."

"That's convenient. So, let's say I believe you work undercover. That means you do things for the Militia and turn the other way when they hurt people."

He frowned. "It's not like that."

"Yes, it is."

"Occasionally, we have to let things go so we can pursue more important targets."

"You make it sound clean and sterile, but we're talking about people's lives here."

He rubbed the heel of his hand against his forehead. She'd noticed him doing that a lot lately. "I know, and it all used to be clear to me. Then you came and I fell in love with you. Now I don't know if I want to be Luke Taylor anymore. I don't know if I can be him."

Jayden struggled to control her breathing. The knot in her throat nearly choked her. If she'd let go of the tears she was trying to keep locked up, she'd be able to breathe. But she had to hang on.

"For the next day or two, you better be Luke Taylor, because I need help and you're it."

"You're going to trust me."

"Of course not. If anything happens to me or the boys, I've left an envelope to be delivered to Paul Dubois. It tells how you've worked with the police and me and hidden things from the Militia. How you've set them all up. You won't last five minutes after he gets that."

Luke nodded. "I see. I help you or you sentence me to death. I already said I'd help. You don't need to threaten me with anything."

"Consider it my insurance policy."

"When they realize I've helped you, they'll kill me anyway."

"You'll get my boys back without them knowing you were involved, if you want to live."

He shook his head. "I don't think that's possible."

"My boys didn't deserve this." For the first time, her voice shook and she couldn't blink back her tears.

Luke's eyes didn't leave her face and she could see the sadness in them. "You're right, they didn't. It doesn't matter about me anyway. I may already have a death sentence from the Militia anyway. We'll find the boys and I'll get you out of this safely. Not because you've threatened me, but because I love you, and them."

He wiped at her tears and she could see his eyelids blink rapidly before he dropped his head to stare at the ground. The fingers that had touched her face now pressed against his closed eyes. She touched his shoulder, unable to forget her feelings for him in spite of his betrayal. "I'd like to believe that, Luke."

Fresh tears spilled over her lashes and beneath her hand he shuddered. "I'm not sure I know you at all. Are you really Luke or is it a cover you've acquired over the years? Who is Luke Taylor?"

He leaned against the wall of the barn. "I've been wondering that myself lately."

"Why do you think you've buried yourself in the Militia?"

"I told you why, because of what happened to me when I was younger, what happened to my mother."

Jayden knotted his shirt in her hand as the tears dried on her face. "I've been thinking about you being in the FBI since last night... You mentioned before that you'd grown up with family in the Militia. I didn't know it was your dad." She paused and Luke didn't move as he waited for her to continue. "Do you ever wonder if going undercover with the Militia was a legitimate way to lead a lifestyle you couldn't let go of?"

Jerking to his full height, his shirt pulled loose from her grasp, and he took a half step away from her. "That's nuts."

"Is it? You told me once you lost someone you loved. Was it because of this?"

He nodded. "Alicia and I worked undercover together. She was killed in a bust."

"Yet you stayed in it."

He stiffened. "I wanted to get them for hurting her."

Jayden frowned at him. "Or did you not know how to function without the Militia? Can you answer that question honestly?"

Even in the dark she could see the flash of anger in Luke's eyes, but he didn't respond.

"That's what I thought. How can I ever know how you feel about the boys because of their race? I don't necessarily trust you to help us, but I think you'll try and save your own skin."

"I'll get the boys back. You can count on that."

She wished he would deny her accusation, even if she didn't think she'd believe him. A sigh slipped past her lips and the exhaustion she'd been avoiding settled on her like a thick quilt making every movement an effort.

"If you're undercover, you're in a lot of danger, more now than ever before. Why have you stayed with it when you could be killed?"

"I thought what I was doing was worth it. Just as falling in love with you was worth the risk. And now getting Garrett and Elliot back is worth the risk, worth my life if it comes to that."

"Let's hope it doesn't." She pushed the note into his hand. "Call me in the morning if you have an idea about what we should do."

There was nothing left to say and she hurried across the yard toward her car. Luke part of the FBI—could she believe him? She wanted to, needed to. She needed his help and his love. Right now she'd settle for the help.

After Jayden left, Luke stayed where he was, resting his back against the rough wooden slats of the barn. He stared at the note she'd given him, without seeing it. His undercover work here was about to end and he'd move on. Was Jayden right? Had he been hell-bent on revenge because it let him remain Militia? He could walk away right now and let the FBI be responsible for getting the boys back. That's what Charles would tell him to do. It was a way to salvage his cover and keep working somewhere else. For years he'd been on the verge of uncovering a very large and secret umbrella organization. Well funded. The names of congressmen and high-ranking officials were frequently linked to it. They were the ones he wanted and with his cover intact he could continue his attempts to expose them.

JAYDEN FORCED HERSELF to put on a calm front as she stepped into the veterinarian clinic the next morning. She wanted things to appear as normal as possible. She'd have to retell the story of her mother's attack a million times. But if the Militia was watching, they would believe she was going along with their plan.

She'd barely started her first cup of coffee when there was a tap on her office door.

"Come in."

Kent stepped inside and Jayden leapt to her feet. "Where the hell have you been? And please tell me Amy is with you."

He hugged her as she threw her arms around him. "Luke sent me here. He said to tell you he'd be by the clinic in an hour with Thor and he'll have what you need."

"He told you."

"You two can't do all of this on your own, Jayden."

"We don't need anyone else involved. You cannot say a word to the police, understand?"

"I understand."

Jayden digested what Kent had said. Luke's arrival with Thor wouldn't raise any suspicions. "Fine. Now, where is Amy?"

"I've taken her to a safe place for now. Bergeron found out about the classes and I had to get her away."

She took Kent's hand. "Thank you for helping her."

"I had to, for both of us. I care about Amy. When I started helping her, well, things escalated pretty quickly."

Leaning against her desk, Jayden smiled for the first time in twenty-four hours. "I'm glad. Now if we can get my boys back and find Walsh, this awful mess will be over."

"You think the Militia will leave you alone?"

"We'll be able to get the police involved after I have my boys."

"I'm not so sure that'll keep you safe. What makes you think anyone will find Walsh alive?"

"We found evidence that he might have gone to a safe house. We don't know where, though." She studied Kent. "You wouldn't know if Duke Swayze had another house somewhere, would you?"

He furrowed his brows in thought. "I don't, but I know who might."

"Amy," they said in unison.

"I'll contact her." Kent turned to the door, but Jayden didn't follow immediately.

"Don't tell Luke anything about Walsh."

Kent turned back to her. "Why?"

"Just don't. He's been neck-deep in the Militia and I know he says he's undercover with the FBI, but I still don't trust him."

"I called the FBI and they verified what Luke said about being undercover."

"How did you know who to call?"

Kent shrugged. "Luke gave me the name."

She arched her eyebrow.

"I still believe him, Jayden."

"You believe whatever you want, but for safety's sake, let's not include him in this."

Kent nodded, shutting her door behind him. Jayden went to her desk and slumped in the chair, her brain already tired from thinking too hard this morning. Kent might trust Luke, but she couldn't afford that luxury.

THE HORSE TRAILER RATTLED behind his truck as Luke pulled into the vet clinic. Jayden met him as he led the horse into the treatment area. She rubbed Thor's nose then fed him a piece of an apple. "What now?"

"I've got a plan."

"No police or FBI, right? They said they'd kill the boys if the police were involved."

"I'm taking care of it, okay?"

He cupped his hand along her cheek. She nearly pulled away then she seemed to flow into him and he had to think to breathe.

"Trust me, Jayden. I won't let you down."

She nodded, her head against his chest. "You look tired," she whispered.

He pushed her back and pulled a computer disk from his pocket. "I didn't sleep. We have plans to make. I made this last night. It took me a while because I couldn't use my computer. I didn't know if they might have bugged it."

"Whose computer did you use?"

He grinned. "I broke into the library."

"You're not serious, are you?"

"Afraid so. But this disk has pictures, notes, everything I could think of that Walsh might have been on to with the Militia. When they check the disk, they'll believe it's from him."

"So what makes them not kill me after they get this?"

"Nothing."

Her eyes widened. "That's not exactly the reassurance I was hoping for."

It wasn't what he'd like to have offered, but at the moment it was the best he could do. "When you get home this evening, take your truck and go behind the house Walsh rented from you. I've left a four-wheeler there and the rails you need to load it on your truck. Drive to your meeting place—it's the old picnic area that was damaged by the flood, right?"

She nodded.

"Leave the truck on the dirt road across the highway and unload the four-wheeler," he continued. "You'll go the rest of the way on it."

"Won't they think it's weird for me to come on that instead of a vehicle I can take the boys away in?"

"They'll figure you have an escape plan. They don't expect you to come in blind and trusting. They know you're smart."

"Okay, so what is the escape plan?"

"Once they look at the disk they'll probably try to kill the three of you. They won't need you then. At that point I'll cause a diversion. You'll jump on the four-wheeler and follow this route." He spread a paper on the counter. "Memorize this because you won't have a map tonight and things look different in the dark. I'll get the boys and we'll make our separate ways down this trail to the river. I've left a boat there and once we're on it we should be able to get away. It's very fast."

"What's this diversion going to be?"

"Something big and loud, so be ready. I want them to think the world is coming to an end."

"And you'll come with us on the boat?"

"I'll be with you."

She tilted her head and studied the paper. "How did you come up with this?"

"It's what I do." He folded the paper and stuck it in her pocket, trying not to let his worry show. Getting them all away safely wouldn't be easy, but he needed Jayden to feel as confident as possible.

"What about the Militia? Is that what you do, too?"

Frowning, he studied the back of his hands. That was the question he'd dealt with all night long. Finally, he pushed a strand of hair away from her face. "You took me aback with that statement last night. For a minute I thought you might be right. But I couldn't let anything happen to you or the boys. That's when I knew I'm not one of them. I did it because I could, because I'm one of the best field agents and in the end I could do good. I'm done now. I don't want to be a part of this lie anymore."

"But you could get there tonight and change your mind."

"I'm not going to do that."

She stepped away from him. "I hope not. But it's a chance I'm going to have to take. At least you're familiar with how the Loyalists operate, and that's what I'm counting on."

Taking Thor's lead, Luke turned the horse around and left Jayden standing in the barn. Even if he got them all out alive she might never trust him again.

## CHAPTER TWENTY-ONE

JEFFREY STUCK HIS HEAD in the door. "Line one is for you."

Dropping the journal she'd been reading, Jayden looked up. "Okay. Slow today, huh?"

He smiled. "Enjoy it. This doesn't happen often."

When Jeffrey left she put the phone to her ear. "This is Jayden."

"Do you know who this is?"

"Yes." She recognized Kent's voice.

"Good, keep it to yourself."

She started to ask him why all this secrecy when she realized he must think her phone line was bugged. Would the Militia go that far? She didn't have time to dwell on it.

"Do you remember where you and I saw a car wreck when we were kids?" Kent asked.

"Of course." She had run into Kent at Haney's old store one afternoon years ago. They'd spent a few hours sitting on the porch steps talking, until a terrible collision happened right in front of them. It wasn't something she'd forget.

"Meet me there in an hour."

"But I'm at work. I can't walk out."

"Find a reason."

The phone went dead. She didn't move for a few seconds then slowly she hung up and got to her feet.

Crossing the hallway, she rapped once then opened the door to Jeffrey's office. He sat at his desk working on the computer.

"I need to leave for the day."

He glanced up. "Anything wrong?"

"Garrett's sick. I have to get him from my cousin's house in Texas." She was surprised at how smoothly the lie rolled off her tongue.

"Sure, go ahead."

She didn't like lying to Jeffrey and after this was all over she'd apologize.

Five minutes later, she steered her car into the gravel parking lot at Haney's. She left her truck as Kent waved to her from a small brown car several yards away. When she reached him he rolled down the window.

"Get in."

She climbed into the passenger seat while Kent cranked the car then pulled onto the highway.

"Wait a minute. Where are we going? I can't leave my truck sitting there."

Kent glanced at her. "It's as safe there as anywhere."

"Hey, Jayden," a soft voice called from the backseat.

She turned to see Amy peeking from under a blanket.

Jayden gaped at Kent. "What's she doing?"

"She's going to help us find that safe house, but I didn't want anyone to know she was here. That's why we're in this rental car and not in mine."

Her heart began to thump at a faster pace and her palms felt cold and damp. How well did she know Kent and Amy? They'd both grown up in the Militia. She gripped the door handle as she glanced at the side of the road, briefly contemplating a leap from the moving vehicle. In the passenger-side mirror she noticed a truck turning onto the same road they'd taken. When Kent made a left, the truck did, too.

"I think there's a truck following us."

Kent glanced in the rearview mirror. "Jackson Cooper. Sheriff Wright couldn't get away."

Jayden spun to face Kent. "What? You didn't tell him about the boys, did you?"

"No, but you can't expect me to take you and Amy to find Duke Swayze's safe house without backup."

"I hope you didn't tell anyone else in the sheriff's office because too many are on the Militia's payroll."

Kent kept his eyes on the road. "Jackson and I know that."

Jayden squinted at the mirror. "Why's he pulling that trailer with the four-wheelers on it?"

"Because you can't get where we're going any other way."

Her heart slowed and she wiped her palms on her khaki pants. Jackson was one person she did trust, though she didn't like the idea of the four of them driving off into the woods not knowing what they would find.

Kent glanced over his shoulder. "Amy, I'll need you to sit up and give me directions from here."

The younger woman leaned over the front seat, one hand on Kent's shoulder and the other pointing forward. "Take the next right."

Kent made the turn.

"Now a left, ahead there."

"That's a dirt road, Amy," Jayden said as the car slowed.

Amy snorted. "It's the last good road you'll see on this trip."

Dust spurted out behind them for a few moments until Amy directed them onto another road that was mostly grass. Could Eric have been living here with no word to anyone for nearly two months? Jayden found it hard to believe. They continued in silence until the road ended at a small field.

"We'll have to take the four-wheelers from here." Amy climbed out of the car.

"Where are we going?" Jayden followed her to Jackson's trailer.

"Duke Swayze's safe house." Amy tugged at the elastic band in her hair.

"How do you know where that is?"

Amy smiled. "I know you think he was nuts but he could be a nice guy. They say he killed some people, but a lot of that was talk. He's my dad's cousin. When I was little and his wife was alive, I stayed with them a lot. He brought me here several times and said it was his secret hiding place. I'd forgotten about it until Kent asked me."

Jackson had brought three ATVs so Amy and Kent rode one together while Jayden and the investigator followed. Crossing the field, they entered a path barely wide enough for them. They bumped along for nearly fifteen minutes before it opened into a clearing with a small brick house in the middle. The windows were barred and the door looked to be solid metal.

Jackson stared at Amy. "How come no one knows about this?"

"He built it himself at night, sneaking materials here. He was always so paranoid."

"How do we get in?" Jayden eyed the bars on the windows.

"He used to keep a key hidden."

They followed her to the side of the house where she bent and ran a hand along the brick near the ground until one moved slightly. She tugged until it slid away from the rest. Tiny spiders ran from the crevice carved into the brick and Amy pulled the key loose.

Jayden shook her head. "I can't believe it."

Amy jiggled the key in the lock and the heavy door creaked open. They walked through the house, but didn't see anyone.

"Doesn't look like he's here." Kent leaned against the kitchen counter.

Frustrated, Jayden toured every room again. If they didn't find Eric here, maybe he was dead.

"Eric, if you're in here, it's Jayden! Come out."

"You think he's hiding?" Kent asked.

"Walsh, this is Jackson Cooper. We've been looking for you." The big man waited a few minutes then shrugged.

From the bedroom, they heard a thump followed by a clang and they raced to the room as the closet door opened and Eric Walsh, thin and pale, stepped from the small space.

Jayden threw her arms around his neck. "I can't believe you're alive. Why didn't you get us word you were okay?"

He glanced at the four of them, his gaze settling on Amy.

"Don't worry," Amy said quickly. "I'm not with Bergeron anymore."

Eric nodded. "Where's Swayze? He locked me in here and left. I could come up here, but all the doors were locked from the outside and with the windows barred I was trapped here. He said I'd be safe, where the Militia couldn't find me. He was supposed to kill me."

Jackson frowned. "Duke Swayze died weeks ago. He hung himself in his jail cell."

At first Eric didn't move, then he stumbled a few steps to the nearest chair and dropped into it. A tiny puff of dust rose around him. His hand covered his mouth. No one spoke. Finally, he shook his head. "He was helping me. Put himself in danger by doing it, but I'd have never gotten all the information I have otherwise. He'd killed one man years ago in self-defense, but the Loyalists like to say he murdered for them. They were burying bodies on his property so he'd look guilty." Eric paused. "I don't believe he killed himself."

"Don't worry, neither do I," Jayden replied.

Eric glanced at her. "I wondered why he didn't come back for so long. I tried to get out, but this place is like a fortress. I'd started thinking I might die here. I figured there was enough food for maybe another month."

"What's down there?" Jackson asked, stepping toward the closet.

"There's a secret door at the back that leads to a basement. That's where Swayze kept food, water—everything he needed to survive for months. He said he was afraid he'd need a place to hide one day so he kept it stocked. There's another living area down there."

"I hope you're ready to leave," Jackson said, indicating the living room.

Eric slowly got to his feet. "I won't go to the sheriff's office and you can't tell anyone you've found me. Too many officers are on the Militia payroll."

"You'll go with me and Amy. She's hiding from the Militia with my parents. You can stay there, too. At least until you decide what else you want to do," Kent said.

Eric nodded and followed them outside, squinting in the bright light. He climbed on the four-wheeler behind Jayden.

"Things could get ugly soon, Jayden."

She looked back at him. "They already have."

With a flick of her wrist she started the engine and ended their conversation.

HOURS LATER, JAYDEN climbed onto the seat of another four-wheeler and thumbed the start switch.

She backed away from the truck and headed to the highway. Crossing the asphalt, she paused on the edge of the gravel road that led to the abandoned picnic area. This was it, Luke's plan. The Militia was probably watching. Swallowing hard she tried to calm her heart that hammered in her chest, then started the machine along the road to the meeting. When she topped the last hill, she could see the reflection of moonlight on the cars below. Headlights came on as she got closer and when she ground the machine to a stop, two of the men waiting jerked her off the seat, roughly patting her down to check for weapons. Surely they didn't think she was dumb enough to wear a gun. After getting the four-wheeler Luke had left for her, she had bought heavy Velcro and attached her pistol in its holster underneath an area between the steering column and the gas tank.

"The vet has arrived." Bergeron stepped in front of her and slammed the weight of his open hand across the side of her face. The force of the blow sent Jayden to her knees where she remained for several seconds.

"That's for holding out on us for so long. You should have turned all evidence over to the police immediately—where we could have gotten it."

Still on the ground, Jayden wiped the back of her hand across her mouth. She tasted blood. "I didn't have it until the other day and didn't think it was important. It doesn't mean anything to me. Where are the boys?"

Bergeron laughed. "As if we can't take that disk from you and never let you see those boys."

As she rolled toward the four-wheeler to get to her

feet, she snaked her hand under the bottom and whipped the gun from its holster. "I grew up shooting pistols and I'm very accurate. Anybody comes to take this disk from me and you get the first bullet." She gripped the gun and got to her feet. "Right between the eyes."

The big man snorted. "I have all these men here and I'll bet they can shoot you and end this."

"Maybe, but not before I get at least one or two rounds off in you."

Bergeron considered her for a second more. "Show her the kids."

Car lights came on, and fifty yards away she could see the boys. Past them was the place where Luke said he'd cut a trail to the river. If he got the boys, they should make it there before her.

"Now give me what you brought."

She pulled the disk Luke had prepared from her jacket pocket. If she'd had time she would have gotten information from Walsh and added it, but Kent had whisked the reporter away immediately. Tossing the disk to Bergeron, she prayed Luke had done a good job with the information on it and that he hadn't double-crossed her. Bergeron handed his prize to another man holding a laptop computer, then smiled.

"Now we wait and hope you haven't tried something stupid."

Jayden prayed Luke hadn't set her up. She'd looked over the information, but the names and notes on it didn't make sense to her—generals, military bases…

"Look at this, boss."

The man behind the computer waved Bergeron over. Jayden held her breath as the big man nodded while eyeing the laptop. He picked it up and walked to a car parked several feet away. The windows were darkened, but as the back passenger window glided down, a flash of light penetrated the interior and her stomach churned.

She swallowed hard to keep from being sick. The man inside moved his head, their eyes met through the open window and he frowned. Jayden took a step toward the car, but one of the men guarding her blocked her path then pushed her backward. With a swift movement, she slammed the barrel of the pistol against the man's forehead and rammed her knee into his groin. Shoving him to the ground, she continued forward. Ahead of her, Joseph Bergeron stepped aside as the car door opened.

The man eased out of the seat, straightening to his full height. Her pistol leveled at his waist as they met toe to toe. The muzzle of Bergeron's gun pressed to her cheek, but the man in front of her brushed it away.

"That's not necessary."

"How could you?" Her voice cracked, but she wouldn't let herself cry. "How could you be part of this?"

General Reginald Arneaux stroked his chin and frowned. "You weren't supposed to see me here, Jayden."

"But I have."

"Yes, so you have."

"You're a Loyalist. Why?"

He gave her a slow smile. "You've been looking for answers since you came back. I guess it's time you got them."

Jayden gripped her pistol tighter. "Yes, it is."

"I'm not a Loyalist. Why would a general who'd spent time at the Pentagon be part of that? We're much bigger, much more connected than the Loyalists."

"Who's we?"

"A group that's so secret most people believe we're simply a conspiracy theory. We exist far enough behind the scenes that no one knows we're there. But we affect policy, make and break candidates, shape the government. Imagine a Militia of true military men, trained by our own military academies."

If she'd ever thought she'd leave here alive, Jayden now realized that General Arneaux would do whatever it took to end her life. Her only hope was Luke's plan.

"Does my mother have any idea?"

He laughed aloud. "Of course not. I only wanted to see if that reporter had left information behind with any of you. She's clueless. Much like you were ten years ago."

She froze except for her index finger twitching on the trigger of the pistol. "Are you telling me you let your own son get killed?"

He shook his head slowly. "You still don't get it, do you? I set the bomb to explode. I planned it. Mark was encouraging Louis to leave and not join the military, not follow the path set for him. Louis should have gone to West Point and one day he could have joined me. But he wanted to throw it all away."

"So you killed them."

"You were supposed to die, too. Dubois wasn't thrilled that his son had to go, but he finally faced the fact that there was no other way. Unfortunate about the banker's daughter, though." He shrugged dismissively.

She took a half step away from him, and out of the corner of her eye, she could see Bergeron's gun still pointed at her.

"You've got what you want, now give me the boys."

Reginald Arneaux started to laugh but it was short-lived as an explosion erupted behind the vehicles. The force of it sent Jayden reeling backward. She squeezed the trigger as she fell and watched the general clutch his right shoulder. Rolling on the ground, she sprung to her feet and ran zigzagging toward the four-wheeler. A bullet whizzed past her ear and she stumbled across the seat and fell on the other side of the ATV. She hit the start button before she was on her feet then slung one leg across the seat. Hitting the gas, she sent the ATV roaring across the park. Another blast lit up the night far ahead of her toward the river and she could make out the opening to the path Luke had shown her on the map. Not far from it she could see one of the men who'd been holding the boys fall from Luke's grasp. Another lay on the ground already. Still gripping his pistol in one hand, Luke snatched the boys, dragging them on his four-wheeler. The flash of light from the blast ended and Jayden could only see blurred figures in the dark as more gunfire erupted behind her.

As a third explosion vibrated the ground, she spotted them again, speeding forward. Garrett was facing Luke, face buried in his chest, and Elliot clung to him from behind. From where she'd just come, she heard Bergeron shout, "Damn you, Taylor!"

She raised her pistol and began to shoot randomly, hoping it would help keep the Militia back until they could get away, even though she knew on the bouncing four-wheeler she couldn't hit a wall. Car engines started behind her as she directed the wheels of the machine onto the tiny trail. Bushes tore at her legs and threatened to knock her off while Jayden prayed she was going the right way.

The trail ended so abruptly she had to turn the handlebars sharply and ended up tipping the four-wheeler on its side to avoid running into the boat at the river's edge. Luke held a flashlight, and she hurried toward him just as the sound of sirens reached her.

"Who called the police?"

"I did. I told you I had this planned."

She planted both feet on the ground. "There weren't supposed to be police. The boys could have gotten killed because of it."

"But they didn't, and you're wasting time. Now get in."

"Did you know?" she shouted as another explosion roared behind them.

"Know what?"

"About Arneaux! Did you know he was part of a secret Militia that's working with the Loyalists?"

This time she had no doubt about Luke's answer. Even in the dim glow of his flashlight she could see the color drain from his face.

"The general is— He told you?"

She nodded.

He didn't move for several seconds then a shout echoed nearby.

"Get in!" The boat rocked as Luke shifted to make room for her. She hesitated. "You still don't trust me."

Dirt and sweat marked his face and she looked at him as the sound of gunfire erupted again from the direction of the park.

"Luke—"

He shook his head as he stepped out of the boat to stand beside her. "I guess I'm not sure what I'm up to right now, either. I can't blame you. In your position I probably wouldn't trust me, either."

He caught the back of her head with his hand and pulled her to him, pressing his lips hard against hers. "I love you, Jayden. Don't forget it."

He shoved her into the boat. "Take the flashlight and get out of here. The Militia will be all over you in about thirty seconds."

She gripped the throttle of the idling boat and when she looked again Luke was gone.

"No!" Elliot screamed and ran to the side of the

boat. She slammed the throttle down, flinging Elliot to the floor. He got to his knees as they bounced across the water, the sleek racing machine moving faster than she'd expected.

Struggling to his knees, Elliot clung to the railing. "You can't leave Luke!" he screamed over the raging motor. She wasn't sure if it was spray from the river hitting her or the wind blowing Elliot's tears.

"We had to!" she shouted back at him.

"No, you didn't. You've killed him!" Still holding on, Elliot turned his face against the side of the boat, his head bumping with each wave, but he didn't seem to care.

She wiped her own wet face with the sleeve of her jacket. She hoped Elliot was wrong. Until Luke had shoved her in the boat and left them, she hadn't known for sure she could trust him. But he'd given up his best chance of escape to make her feel safer and still been able to say he loved her, to understand her fear. She glanced back toward the bank they'd left, but it was too far away to see anything. Oh, God, what had she done to him?

## CHAPTER TWENTY-TWO

LUKE SHOVED HIS CELL PHONE back in his pocket. A thin tree limb whipped against his face as he struggled to see shapes through the dark. He gave up and, instead, tried to visualize the lay of the land. He'd scouted the area in the predawn hours for the best escape route. He'd nixed the idea of going this way on foot but was glad now he'd at least walked through here. It wouldn't have worked with the kids, but alone he had a chance. Splashing into the creek that fed the river, he wished he'd been able to ride his four wheeler this far but the growth had been too thick. Besides, escaping on foot was quieter and upped his odds. He could hear shouts not far behind him as he headed upstream.

He'd hoped Jayden would believe in him, but she hadn't and he couldn't blame her. He'd lied at every turn. He loved the boys and he didn't care about their background. He only cared about them. He was ready to give up his career to be with them. A light flashed in the bush and he grunted then dropped into the water, taking a deep breath before he submerged himself. He held on to a sunken tree trunk beside him. At the moment giving this up wasn't such a bad idea. Besides, he'd had a member of the secret Militia he'd been after for most of his career right under his nose for two years and he'd never known. What kind of undercover agent did that make him? Maybe Walsh had found out and that was why he was missing.

Luke readjusted his grip on the tree trunk and wondered exactly how long he could hold his breath. Ignoring the burning in his lungs, he watched lights flash above the water. He brought his face to the surface, gasped in air, then went under again.

He came up for air two more times before he felt it was safe to lift his entire head out of the water. He could hear shouting but it was farther away and he didn't see any lights. He got to his feet and continued to splash up the creek. Ahead, he could see the shadow of a bridge. A car passed slowly but he couldn't tell the make. Moving closer to the side of the road, he waited in the brush and in a few minutes it passed again, followed by two trucks. On its third pass, the car stopped in the middle of the bridge and the driver got out.

"Luke, where are you?"

He recognized Kent's voice immediately and rushed up the embankment. Sliding into the backseat, he lay on the floorboard.

"Let's go, Kent."

The younger man pushed the gas and the car shot forward.

"You better be glad your cell phone worked here so I'd know to come and meet you. Did Jayden and the boys make it out okay?"

Luke tried to find a more comfortable position. "I think so. They were heading upriver in the boat the last time I saw them."

"And you should have gone with them."

"She didn't trust me. She thought I'd lead them straight to the Militia again. Besides, it helped draw attention away from them when we separated."

Kent glanced back at him. "I guess you can't blame her for not trusting you."

Luke took a deep breath. "No, I can't. And don't look back here."

The younger man was silent for a few minutes. "So what happens now?"

"Lots more arrests, I hope. Then I move on to become someone else."

"So you're not Luke Taylor, huh?"

"No, I'm not."

"That must be pretty hard, to pretend all the time. Don't you ever forget who you are?"

Luke moved from the floor to the backseat, keeping his head below the window as lights passed them on the road. Ahead he could see a police road block.

"Yeah, until recently, I think I had forgotten."

"So did Cypress Landing bring out the real Luke Taylor?"

"Maybe so, maybe it was this place and the people here."

"Or could it have been one person in particular?"

Luke laughed. "That, too, I think. But she'll never believe I wasn't undercover with the Militia to feed some deep need I had to be part of them."

"Were you?"

"No, I wasn't. I needed to stop them and their hatred. Undercover seemed the best way and I was the best person to do it."

Kent slowed to a stop at the road block. "Looks like you pulled this one off. Now that they have the Militia for kidnapping and with all the information that Walsh has given them, you and Jayden don't have to worry about anyone coming after you."

Luke leaned over the front seat. "What did you say?"

"I said you won't have to worry about the Militia being after you."

"No, about Walsh."

"Oh!" Kent turned to face him. "Jayden wouldn't let me tell you earlier today, but we found Walsh. She still wasn't sure you would keep it from the Militia."

"How did you find him?"

"The clue was in Elliot's notebook, then Amy helped us."

Sliding quietly from the car, Luke still didn't believe the answer had been in Elliot's hands all this time and they hadn't found it. He could see Charles Greer waiting for him among the officers at the road block. This would be one of the biggest Militia busts ever and he wasn't sure he'd done anything to cause it. He had, however, sacrificed more than he wanted to consider in the process.

JAYDEN BARELY PUSHED the accelerator as she rolled along the driveway to Luke's house. She'd heard he'd escaped without injury. She'd also heard he was moving on to a new assignment. She'd heard a lot of things. Stopping the car, she sat for a few seconds. After two days of secondhand information about Luke, she'd decided she had to see him. She'd made up her mind that she didn't want to live without him, didn't want him to leave. Not without her and the boys. But he led a life of secrecy and danger. Could he do that and be with them? Would he even want to? She'd left him on that riverbank to fend for himself while he'd done everything he could to make them safe. He'd likely toss her straight out of his house. But she had to know if there was a chance, because she never thought she'd love someone like she loved Luke.

Forcing herself from the car, she went to the door, which stood open. The backseat of the four-door truck was stacked with boxes and suitcases. He was leaving without saying goodbye. She paused then pushed forward again. Inside the house, down the hall, she followed the sound of drawers opening and closing until she stood in the doorway of Luke's bedroom.

His back was to her and she wished this didn't have to be so hard, that their lives could be simpler. Then he spun around, T-shirts in his hands.

"Jayden."

"Luke." He looked surprised to see her, but not angry. "You're leaving."

He glanced around the room. "Yes, I'm going to a new job."

"Were you going to say goodbye?"

"I don't know. I hadn't decided yet. I wasn't sure if you'd want me to."

Silence hung between them and she shifted her weight from one foot to the other. "Who are you, really?"

"Luke Sanders, from Alabama."

She nodded. "Who will you be later?"

"I'll always be Luke Sanders. I always have been. The name changes, but I don't."

"Well, where will you go?"

He tossed the T-shirts on the bed. "What difference does it make, and what's up with the twenty questions? Why are you here, Jayden? To say goodbye, to tell me you don't trust me, what?"

Her throat tightened and her vision blurred. She wasn't supposed to cry and get all emotional.

"I'm asking because—" she paused to sniff and clear her throat "—because I want to know where you'll be, who you'll be. I'd like to come see you wherever it is you're going, maybe bring the boys. If you were going to be there for a long time, like you were here, we could move there, too. You could still be undercover and do your job."

She stopped. She was blathering on and on. Luke's face was expressionless and she didn't know what to do next.

"Are you saying you and the boys would move anyplace I'm sent so we can be together? Is that what you're saying?"

"Yes."

"Why would you do that?"

"Because I love you. The boys love you—we love you."

"Did the boys send you here?"

She frowned. "They're kids, they don't send me anywhere. But I know they love you as much as I do and that's a lot."

"What about trust? Do you trust me?"

"Implicitly."

"How can I be sure?"

She smiled slightly. "You'd have to trust me. But you've proven yourself as far as I'm concerned. I'm willing to do whatever's necessary to prove my trust to you."

He nodded slowly, and she waited for what would come next.

"And you'd follow me even to, say, Boston?"

"Yes."

"Northern Maine?"

"It's cold there and I don't like cold, but yes, I'd go there, too."

He took a few steps toward her then paused. "What about Montana?"

He was watching her closely and she tried to clear her throat. It was hard for her to speak, so she bobbed her head instead.

"South Florida, what about there?"

"That's a better option, yes, definitely."

He stepped closer until he was only inches away. "What about South America?"

"That's another continent, Luke. The FBI is not going to send you to South America."

"They might. Would you go?"

"Yes, I'd go to South America."

He pulled her to him, crushing her against his chest. "You must be nuts, woman."

"I am, about you."

"Good, because I'm nuts about you."

He lowered his mouth to hers and kissed her until she clung to the front of his shirt for support. He shoved the bedroom door shut and flipped the lock, then peeled off his T-shirt, tossing it to the floor.

Jayden grinned and did the same, her shirt landing on top of his. He lifted her and carried her to the bed.

"So where are you going? The truth this time," she asked as he dropped her on top of the covers.

"Nowhere. I have to get my own house, though. The FBI isn't going to pay for this if I don't work for them, and I can't afford this place as a public defender."

Jayden jerked to her knees. "What are you talking about?"

"I quit the FBI. I'm staying here and I'll be the public defender. Seems they have an opening now and I am a lawyer, you know. That part was true."

He pulled her on top of him. "Now shut up and kiss me."

And she did.

\* \* \* \* \*

Kimberley Blackstone didn't notice the waiting horde of media until it was too late. Flashbulbs exploded around her like a New Year's light show. She skidded to a halt, so abruptly her trailing suitcase all but overtook her.

This had to be a case of mistaken identity. Surely. Kimberley hadn't been on the paparazzi hit list for close to a decade, not since she'd estranged herself from her billionaire father and his headline-hungry diamond business.

But no, it was *her* name they called. *Her* face was the focus of a swarm of lenses that circled her like avid hornets. Her heart started to pound with fear-fueled adrenaline.

What did they want?

What was going on?

With a rising sense of bewilderment she scanned the crowd for a clue, and her gaze fastened on a tall, leonine figure forcing his way to the front. A tall, familiar figure. Her head came up in stunned recognition, and their gazes collided across the sea of heads before the cameras erupted with another barrage of flashes, this time right in her exposed face.

Blinded by the flashbulbs—and by the shock of that momentary eye-meet—Kimberley didn't realize his intent until he'd forged his way to her side, possibly by the sheer strength of his personality. She felt his arm wrap around her shoulder, pulling her into the protective shelter of his body, allowing her no time to object. No chance to lift her hands to ward him off.

In the space of a hastily drawn breath, she found herself plastered knee-to-nose against six feet two inches of hard-bodied male.

Ric Perrini.

Her lover for ten torrid weeks, her husband for ten tumultuous days.

Her ex for ten tranquil years.

After all this time, he should not have felt so familiar but, oh dear, he did. She knew the scent of that body and its lean, muscular strength. She knew its heat and its slick power and every response it could draw from hers.

She also recognized the ease with which he'd taken control of the moment and the decisiveness of his deep voice when it rumbled close to her ear. "I have a car waiting outside. Is this your only luggage?"

Kimberley nodded. "I assume you will tell me," she said tightly, "what this welcome party is all about."

"Not while the welcome party is within earshot. No."

Barking a request for the cameramen to stand aside, Perrini took her hand and pulled her into step with his ground-eating stride. Kimberley let him, because he was right, damn his arrogant, Italian-suited hide. Despite the speed with which he whisked her across the airport terminal, she could almost feel the hot breath of the pursuing media on her back.

This was neither the time nor the place for explanations. Inside his car, however, she would get answers.

Now that the initial shock had been blown away— by the haste of their retreat, by the heat of her gathering indignation, by the rush of adrenaline fired by Perrini's presence and the looming verbal battle— her brain was starting to tick over. This had to be her father's doing. And if it was a Howard Blackstone publicity ploy, then it had to be about Blackstone Diamonds, the company that ruled his life.

The knowledge made her chest tighten with a familiar ache of disillusionment.

She'd known her father would be flying in from Sydney for today's opening of the newest in his chain of exclusive, high-end jewelry boutiques. The opulent shopfront sat adjacent to the rival business where Kimberley worked. No coincidence, she thought bitterly, just as it was no coincidence that Ric Perrini was here in Auckland ushering her to his car.

Perrini was Howard Blackstone's right-hand man, second in command at Blackstone Diamonds, a legacy of his short-lived marriage to the boss's daughter. No doubt her father had sent him to fetch her; the question was *why?*

\* \* \* \* \*

*Get swept away down under with the glitz
and glamour of the Blackstone empire as
Kimberley tries to determine the real reason
behind her "reunion" with Ric....*

*Look for*
*VOWS & A VENGEFUL GROOM*
*By Bronwyn Jameson*
*In stores January 2008*

When Kimberley Blackstone's father is
presumed dead, Kimberley is required to take
over the helm of Blackstone Diamonds. She
has to work closely with her ex, Ric Perrini, to
battle not only the press, but also the fierce
attraction still sizzling between them. Does Ric
feel the same...or is it the power her share of
Blackstone Diamonds will provide him as he
battles for boardroom supremacy.

**Look for**

# VOWS &
# A VENGEFUL GROOM

**by**

# BRONWYN
# JAMESON

*Available January wherever you buy books*

# REQUEST YOUR FREE BOOKS!
## 2 FREE NOVELS PLUS 2 FREE GIFTS!

HARLEQUIN®

*Super Romance*®

## Exciting, emotional, unexpected!

**YES!** Please send me 2 FREE Harlequin Superromance® novels and my 2 FREE gifts. After receiving them, if I don't wish to receive any more books, I can return the shipping statement marked "cancel." If I don't cancel, I will receive 6 brand-new novels every month and be billed just $4.69 per book in the U.S., or $5.24 per book in Canada, plus 25¢ shipping and handling per book and applicable taxes, if any*. That's a savings of close to 15% off the cover price! I understand that accepting the 2 free books and gifts places me under no obligation to buy anything. I can always return a shipment and cancel at any time. Even if I never buy another book from Harlequin, the two free books and gifts are mine to keep forever.          135 HDN EEX7  336 HDN EEYK

| | |
|---|---|
| Name | (PLEASE PRINT) |

| | |
|---|---|
| Address | Apt. |

| | | |
|---|---|---|
| City | State/Prov. | Zip/Postal Code |

Signature (if under 18, a parent or guardian must sign)

Mail to the **Harlequin Reader Service®**:
**IN U.S.A.:** P.O. Box 1867, Buffalo, NY 14240-1867
**IN CANADA:** P.O. Box 609, Fort Erie, Ontario L2A 5X3

Not valid to current Harlequin Superromance subscribers.

**Want to try two free books from another line?**
**Call 1-800-873-8635 or visit www.morefreebooks.com.**

* Terms and prices subject to change without notice. NY residents add applicable sales tax. Canadian residents will be charged applicable provincial taxes and GST. This offer is limited to one order per household. All orders subject to approval. Credit or debit balances in a customer's account(s) may be offset by any other outstanding balance owed by or to the customer. Please allow 4 to 6 weeks for delivery.

**Your Privacy:** Harlequin is committed to protecting your privacy. Our Privacy Policy is available online at www.eHarlequin.com or upon request from the Reader Service. From time to time we make our lists of customers available to reputable firms who may have a product or service of interest to you. If you would prefer we not share your name and address, please check here. ☐

HSR07

# *Inside* ROMANCE

Stay up-to-date on all your
romance reading news!

*Inside Romance* is a FREE quarterly newsletter
highlighting our upcoming series releases
and promotions.

Visit
**www.eHarlequin.com/InsideRomance**
to sign up to receive our complimentary newsletter today!

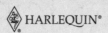

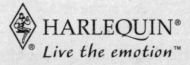

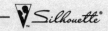

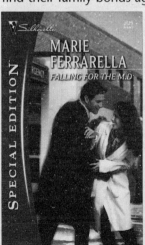

# COMING NEXT MONTH

**#1464 DEAL ME IN • Cynthia Thomason**
*Texas Hold 'Em*
Brady Carrick thought that by accepting his father's bet, he'd upset the lives
of single mom Molly Davis and her son for good. Turns out the small-town
waitress has an ulterior motive, and it is Brady's life that's about to take a
dramatic twist. Because when it comes to love, the stakes are high....

**#1465 CAITLIN'S COWBOY • Barbara McMahon**
*Home on the Ranch*
Caitlin is down on her luck, and she's in Wyoming for one reason only—to
sell the ranch her distant relation unexpectedly left her and get out of town.
But the beauty of the ranch that has been in her family for generations starts to
get under her skin—just like the sole remaining cowboy, Zack Carson.

**#1466 HOW TO TRAP A PARENT • Joan Kilby**
Movie publicist Jane Linden returns to Red Hill, eager to sell her late aunt's
farm and cut all ties with the town she fled, pregnant and alone, twelve years
earlier. If only the local real estate agent wasn't her former high school sweetheart…
and their respective kids weren't conniving to help them fall in love again.

**#1467 A PERFECT STRANGER • Terry McLaughlin**
Mr. Perfect-on-Paper versus the perfect stranger. Henry Barlow is an attorney
with a beautiful home, solid investment portfolio and a ring in hand. Nick
Martelli is tall, dark and devilishly dangerous. When forced to make the
choice, how can Sydney Gordon decide which man is the right one for her?

**#1468 THE MISSING MOM • Ann Evans**
*A Little Secret*
It's been eight years since Maggie Tillman laid eyes on Will Stewart, her first
love. Now a successful architect, he'll never know what their breakup cost her.
But Will is hiding his own secret...a secret that could cost him both his adopted
daughter and a second chance with Maggie once she discovers the truth....

**#1469 RETURN TO EMMETT'S MILL • Kimberly Van Meter**
When Natasha Simmons left Emmett's Mill, she had no intention of ever
returning. Fate, however, intervened and now she's back. Worse, Josh Halvorsen,
her former high school sweetheart, is home, too, and she's even more torn
because there's still a spark between them. But is that reason enough to stay in
a town that holds nothing but bad memories?